ELLIOT JELLY-LEGS AND THE BOBBLEHEAD MIRACLE

A novel

Yolanda Ridge

Illustrated by Sydney Barnes

ORCA BOOK PUBLISHERS

Published in Canada and the United States in 2023 by Orca Book Publishers.
orcabook.com

Library and Archives Canada Cataloguing in Publication
Title: Elliot Jelly-Legs and the bobblehead miracle : a novel /
Yolanda Ridge ; illustrations by Sydney Barnes.
Names: Ridge, Yolanda, 1973- author. | Barnes, Sydney, illustrator.
Identifiers: Canadiana (print) 20220185468 | Canadiana (ebook) 20220185492 |
ISBN 9781459833791 (softcover) | ISBN 9781459833807 (PDF) |
ISBN 9781459833814 (EPUB)
Classification: LCC PS8635.I374 E45 2023 | DDC jC813/.6—dc23

Library of Congress Control Number: 2022934492

Summary: In this illustrated middle-grade novel, eleven-year-old Elliot relies on his Carey Price bobblehead doll to help him excel on his hockey team.

Orca Book Publishers is committed to reducing the consumption of nonrenewable resources in the production of our books. We make every effort to use materials that support a sustainable future.

Orca Book Publishers gratefully acknowledges the support for its publishing programs provided by the following agencies: the Government of Canada, the Canada Council for the Arts and the Province of British Columbia through the BC Arts Council and the Book Publishing Tax Credit.

Cover and interior design by Sydney Barnes
Edited by Tanya Trafford

Printed and bound in Canada.

26 25 24 23 • 1 2 3 4

For Spencer. Thank you for turning me into a hockey mom and showing me what determination can accomplish.

Don't be discouraged from the improbable.
—Carey Price

CHAPTER 1

"It's the most important penalty shot of the season."

Duncan points his plastic mini stick at me before continuing in a deep sportscaster voice.

"Star goalie for the red team, Elliot Feldner-Martel, crouches into position. The outcome of the game rests entirely on his shoulders."

Feet planted, I sink lower and narrow my eyes at my best friend. He keeps talking as he rushes toward me. "Duncan Bilenki, lead scorer for the blue team, stickhandles into the zone. He dekes to the right, waits for the goalie to commit, then snaps a laser toward the open side—"

My legs feel like they're being ripped in half as one socked foot slides away from the other. I'm a millisecond too late. The ball curves past my outstretched pad into the small net behind me.

"—and scores!" Duncan pumps his fist.

"I wasn't ready!" I shout, even though I was totally ready. The angle of Duncan's shot was as obvious as an illegal cross-check. I should've blocked it. He had even told me what he was going to do. Not that he needed to—I know all his moves.

We play hockey pretty much every day. When it's too cold to play in the street, like today, we play mini sticks in Duncan's basement.

It's only September, but the rain outside is thick enough to resurface an ice sheet. We've been shooting a tennis ball at each other with our mini sticks for so long that the high windows of the basement are covered in steam.

"Reset!" I scramble to my feet and pull the ball out of the netting, tugging harder than I need to.

Duncan taps his stick against his palm. "Attention, sports fans," he announces to our imaginary audience, "there will now be a short delay while Feldner-Martel does his famous Patrick Roy routine."

This is Duncan's way of complaining about how long it takes me to get set. It might bug me if someone else said it, but with Duncan I don't mind. Duncan gets away with a lot of things I wouldn't put up with from others. There's something about him—he wins over everyone he meets, and he's good at everything he does. A couple years ago some of the hockey kids started calling him Can Can after someone said, "If anyone can do it Dun-can can." It's true.

"Patrick Roy's not the only NHL superstar who's superstitious," I say as I line the net up with the floor tiles. "Sid the Kid wouldn't call his mom on game days. The Great One refused to get his hair cut on the road. And Glenn 'Mr. Goalie' Hall used to throw up before every game—"

"On purpose!" Duncan finishes with a grin.

I hit my blocker three times before tapping each goalpost in the exact same spot I tapped last time. I don't talk to my goalposts like Patrick Roy did, but I feel less alone in net when I remind myself the goalposts are there. Leaning back until I can feel the crossbar behind me, I take a deep breath, shake my head and narrow my eyes at Duncan to get focused. "I'm ready. Bring it on."

"Want to switch?" he asks.

Both of us like playing goal, so we always split our time in net. I've already gone through my whole goalie routine, though. "One more. Then we'll switch."

Duncan nods to make sure I'm ready before pushing the tennis ball forward with his stick. I come out to challenge. He unleashes a slap shot. From my knees, I throw up a blocker. It looks like the ball's going to beat me top shelf, but at the last second I snag it with my glove.

"Great save, Elliot!" Duncan's dad stands at the bottom step, clapping. He's still dressed in his Canada Post uniform. "You've got good hands."

DUNCAN BILENKI
Can Can • Defense
TRAIL BLAZERS
4

"Thanks, Coach Matt." My tongue trips a little on the word *Coach*. I've known Duncan's dad almost as long as I've known Duncan—since kindergarten, when he let me borrow a stick so I could play street hockey with him and his cousins instead of just watching—yet I still don't know what to call him. He doesn't want me to call him Mr. Bilenki. But it feels weird to call him Matt. Besides, my dad would kill me if he heard me refer to any adult by their first name.

When Duncan's dad coached our hockey team last year, everyone called him Coach Matt. That felt right. Except now we're in his basement, not at the rink.

"Sorry to interrupt you, boys," he says, picking up the remote, "but the game's on."

The big screen flickers to life, and Coach Matt's glasses explode with color. He rubs his hands together like he's about to dive into a bowl full of candy. "Everyone at work was talking about this preseason matchup between Vancouver and Calgary. I bet the whole town will be tuning in."

He's probably right. Since Trail is halfway between Vancouver and Calgary, people who live here either cheer for the Canucks or the Flames. There's the odd Oilers fan too, which keeps things interesting.

As the pre-game analysis cuts to commercial, Duncan's dad mutes the TV and flops down on the couch. "So are you excited about hockey season starting, Elliot?"

"Course." I try to sound casual as a bead of sweat trickles down the back of my neck. I'm actually a bit nervous about moving up to U13—where everyone will be even bigger and faster than they were in U11—but mostly I'm pumped about getting a second chance to prove myself.

My mom and dad didn't sign me up for hockey when I was younger. Mom was worried about concussions. Dad said it was too expensive. I think the real reason was that we were all too busy with other stuff. They were probably hoping I'd lose interest too. I never did. Last year—when things opened up after a year of no extracurricular activities at all—they finally caved and let me play.

I felt like I'd won the lottery.

But then I got on the ice.

Even though I was a pro at mini sticks and street hockey, there was a problem. Just a small one.

I couldn't skate.

I worked to catch up, desperately trying to close the gap between me and my teammates (who could skate before they could walk). I went to every public skate I could. Most of the time the ice was too crowded for me to work on my edges and practice hockey stops. So I watched how-to videos on YouTube and practiced by sliding across my bedroom carpet in my socks. But no matter how hard I tried, I was always at the end of the line in every drill. And when it came to games, I was always in the wrong zone because I couldn't keep up with the play.

This season things will be different. I'm sure of it.

An aerial shot of Rogers Arena appears on the screen, and Coach Matt unmutes the TV. "Come to think of it, I'm not sure I saw your name on the registration list, Elliot."

"Huh." My heart thumps so loudly I'm sure Duncan and his dad can hear it over the TV. My parents promised to sign me up! And I wrote the early-bird registration deadline on the calendar in permanent red marker so they wouldn't forget. "I'll check with my mom," I say, trying to sound like it is no big deal.

Duncan pulls on his Vancouver Canucks jersey over his damp T-shirt and plunks down next to his dad. "Hey, Dad, did you order pizza?"

He nods. "Mediterranean and Pepperoni Classic. Enough for Elliot too."

My mouth waters as the opening notes of the national anthem flood the basement. "Thanks, but I told Mom I'd be home for dinner."

As much as I want pizza, there's no time to waste. I have to get home and convince Mom and Dad to sign me up for hockey before it's too late. Otherwise I'll be left behind. Again.

CHAPTER 2

When I get home, Mom's in the kitchen. She's talking into her headset as she makes dinner.

My sister's sitting at the counter reading a book—*How to Teach Your Dog Quantum Mechanics*. This makes no sense, especially since we don't have a dog. And even if we did, why would a dog need to know physics?

"Aislyn, where's Dad?" I ask. He's usually in his studio, but I don't hear any noise coming from downstairs.

She answers without looking up. "Meeting with some people who want him to do a special carving for their yard."

Perfect. This is my chance to ask Mom about hockey. But she's so deep in conversation, she barely notices me as I motion for her to hang up. The pot on the stove looks dangerously close to boiling over. I give the water a stir.

Waiting would be easier if I could watch the game. But my parents refuse to pay for the sports channel. Or any channel. The only *screen time* they allow is for video games, because Mom read somewhere that it helps kids with hand-eye coordination and problem-solving.

"Want to play *NHL All-Stars*?" I ask Aislyn.

"I'm reading," she replies. "Duh."

"That's a book? I thought it was your face."

We both laugh. Jokes about how much my sister reads are pretty common in our house. Before we adopted her, she had bounced from place to place in foster care with a suitcase crammed full of books instead of clothes.

Mom finally ends her call, takes out her earbuds and pinches the bridge of her nose. I know she only does this when she's really stressed.

"Need some help, Mom?"

Not that I would be much help. When it comes to cooking, none of us know what we're doing. The kitchen is Dad's domain. But I shred some cheese as Aislyn watches over the noodles, and after twenty minutes of total chaos, we sit down at the table with bowls full of something that resembles macaroni and cheese.

Now I can finally ask Mom about hockey. Just as I'm about to bring it up, she turns to my sister and asks her about school. Aislyn starts filling us in on every detail of her totally boring day.

I want to scream. Instead I start balancing my chair on two legs—practically daring Mom to interrupt my sister and tell me to stop. But Aislyn's bragging about acing the math test we had today, so Mom doesn't even notice.

"How did you do on the test, honey?" Mom asks, finally turning her attention to me.

Great.

My sister and I are the same age. And even though we're in the same grade, we're not in the same class. Aislyn gets really good marks. Me, not so much. So Mom asked them to separate us after she and Dad had a big fight about whether being together was bad for my self-esteem (Mom's opinion) or a good way to motivate me to do better (Dad's opinion). But this year both sixth-grade classes are doing math together, so separating us wasn't an option, except when they divide us into groups of *needs more practice* and *ready to move on*.

I blow the air out of my cheeks. "Okay. I got 75."

"Aislyn got 100 percent and you only got 75?" Dad asks as he walks into the kitchen. "Did you study at all?"

My chair hits the floor with a thud.

"Let's not get into this now," Mom says as Dad lifts the lid to see what's left in the pot on the stove. "I was waiting for you to get home before telling them—"

Aislyn sets down her fork. "Telling us what?"

"Mom has good news." Dad puts the lid back on and grabs one of his premade smoothies from the fridge. "Go on, then."

Mom sits up a little straighter and grins at us. "I've decided to run for mayor."

"What? Why?" When Dad said "good news," I was hoping for something like a teachers' strike or an extra month of summer holidays.

"Perhaps you should start with congratulations, E?" I can tell by Dad's tone that he's disappointed.

Before I can react the way he wants me to, Aislyn jumps in. "Congratulations, Mom!" She waves pretend pom-poms in the air, acting like Mom's been nominated for president of the world. "Is this so you can fight the urban-farming bylaw?"

"Of course." I hit my forehead with the palm of my hand. "The chickens." Mom's store sells all kinds of local stuff, including honey and eggs. For years she's been fighting a bylaw that forbids beekeeping and backyard chickens.

"Yes, it's partly about the chickens. But there are other issues I want to address as well."

"This is a great opportunity for your mother. It's going to take support from the whole family." Dad takes a big gulp of his smoothie. As his words sink in, what's left of my appetite vanishes.

"Which means there are going to be some changes around here," says Mom. "To start with, you two can only sign up for one extracurricular activity each."

Aislyn and I both speak at the same time.

"The Change Climate Change contest," Aislyn says.

"Hockey," I say.

Dad's response is immediate. "Not hockey."

The cheese in my stomach curdles. "*Why not?*"

"Too much time. Too much money—" By the way he's using his fingers to list off the reasons, I can tell Dad's just getting started. But I'm not going to give up just yet.

"Duncan's dad will drive me," I say. "And I'll help pay. I can work at the store. Or apply for one of those grants Coach mentioned."

Dad shoots me a look. "I'm surprised you want to play that badly, E. By the end of last year you had as good as given up."

Heat pricks my ears. "I HAD NOT!"

Mom touches my arm. The weight of her hand calms me down. Sometimes I need to work on controlling what Mom used to call my Big Bad Wolf emotions. Huffing and puffing never gets me what I want, especially since we adopted Aislyn, who's always so calm and *reasonable*. So I try counting to ten in my head and taking deep breaths like Mom taught me.

She turns to Dad. "We said one activity each, Jack. If this is what Elliot wants to do, we'll make it work."

"It's too expensive." Dad folds his hands on the table like a judge. "He will probably need new equipment. And we've already missed the early-bird deadline."

I can see the big red circle I drew on the calendar from where I'm sitting. I blink and it multiplies, rushing at me like a mob of angry emojis. They didn't *miss* the deadline. They *ignored* it.

My fists tighten into balls. Containing all the emotion bubbling inside me is like holding in a fart—I'm about to burst from the pressure.

"Besides, it's not just the registration fees," Dad continues. "It's the jersey deposit and the tournament costs and the team fees…remember how it all added up last year?"

Aislyn and I exchange glances. Things always get tense when Mom and Dad talk about money, especially since they lost their accountant. That's when Mom took over bookkeeping for both the store and Dad's wood-carving business and put Dad in charge of household expenses.

"I'm sure I can convince the league to honor the early-bird price," Mom says to Dad. "Is there enough money in the account to cover that for now?"

Silence settles over the kitchen. I cross and uncross my fingers behind my back like I always do when Mom and Dad argue about me. I have to do it three times, starting with my right hand, or things won't go my way.

The clock above the sink ticks like a bomb. It feels like my life is on the line as I cross and uncross my fingers three more times.

Finally Dad clears his throat. "I'll crunch the numbers and let you know."

CHAPTER 3

I spend the next week waiting for Dad to crunch the numbers. It's so painful, he might as well be crunching my toes.

Just when I'm starting to feel as desperate as a free agent in a scoring drought, an email arrives. My registration has been accepted. Dates and instructions for evaluations are attached.

There are no tryouts in house league. Everyone who signs up gets to play. The coaches do their best to divide players so that all the teams—there's always at least three or four of them—are evenly matched.

"I guess your dad must've sold one of his big wooden bear carvings or something," Duncan says. I told him about the email as soon as it arrived, but we're still talking about it over lunch the next day—that's how relieved I am.

The cafeteria is unusually quiet, probably because it's finally sunny outside. I lower my voice. "Maybe. But I don't really think it's about money."

It's true we aren't rich, but it's not like we've ever had our electricity cut off. That happened to my old babysitter sometimes when her parents couldn't pay the bills. Mom's store doesn't bring in a lot of cash, but we do okay. I know I'm lucky to have things like video games and an endless supply of books that I can read in my own bedroom that's decorated with all the hockey stuff my grandpa has sent me over the years. One time we even got to travel all the way to Montreal to visit my grandparents.

"When I thanked my parents for signing me up, Dad gave me a list of terms and conditions longer than one of those computer privacy things." I spread out my fingers and start pointing to each one as I try to imitate Dad's British accent. "Be a good sport, keep up your grades, pitch in around the house, listen to your mother, don't argue with your sister—I swear, breathing wrong could get me booted out of hockey." I throw my hands in the air. "My dad just hates sports."

Duncan stops laughing. "What do you mean? How can anyone hate sports?"

I shrug. "Mom thinks it's because his brother got so much attention for playing soccer."

"Soccer's a big deal in England. Was his brother any good?" Duncan asks through a bite of ham sandwich.

"No idea." I wish I knew the answer, but Dad never talks about his family. I've never even met them. I don't complain about it, though, because I get to talk to my other grandpa all the time over video chat. Duncan doesn't even get to see his mom.

"Why aren't you dorks outside playing b-ball with everyone else?" I turn to see Hunter Reid standing behind us, carrying a basketball.

HUNTER REID

30   GOALIE   TRAIL BLAZERS

Hunter's in seventh grade, so I don't know him that well. Not as well as Duncan anyway. Hunter played goal for Duncan's U11 team when he was a first-year and Hunter was a second. Their dads sometimes arrange extra ice time so they can have one-on-one practice; super shooter against great goalie.

Duncan points to the textbook sitting open in front of him. "We're cramming for a math test this afternoon."

Hunter spins the basketball between his palms. "Seriously? It's only September."

Duncan shrugs. "September marks count just as much as December marks."

"Whatever," says Hunter. "Why aren't you trying out for rep this season, Can Can?"

"You know me. I just play for fun," Duncan replies. "Are you trying out?"

"Just for practice." Hunter stares at his basketball like it's the most interesting thing in the world. He's never been good enough to make rep—in Trail there's only one team of all-stars for each age group—yet his dad makes him try out every year. I'm sure it's good practice, but it must suck to keep getting cut. Embarrassed for him, I stuff the rest of my banana in my mouth and concentrate on chewing.

"So we'll see you at house evaluations next week?" Duncan asks Hunter.

"Both of you?" Hunter turns his attention to me for the first time. "Didn't you get enough of crawling around on the ice last season, Jelly?"

The nickname Jelly—short for Jelly-Legs or Jelly-Knees, referring to the general way I can't seem to stand up straight on the ice—bugged me a lot last year. Still, it was better than Bambi or Feldner-Falls-A-Lot or any of the other nicknames they tried out on me. And in a way it made me feel included.

Being called Jelly now—by someone who doesn't even know me—sounds like a curse.

"You're the one who'll be crawling on the ice after I roof the puck over your shoulder," says Duncan.

Duncan's comeback takes away a bit of the sting. I crack a smile and take a gulp of milk.

One of Hunter's buddies comes up behind him and knocks the ball out from under his elbow.

My smile grows wider.

"Hey!" Hunter turns and chases after his friend or the ball—it's not clear which.

We turn back to our books. "Did you study at all last night?" Duncan asks.

I shake my head. "It's bad luck to study the night before the exam."

"Another superstition?" Duncan smiles. "Good thing you didn't walk under any ladders or cross paths with a black cat either."

I laugh. "Those are more like bad omens than superstitions."

"You're superstitious, huh?"

Darn. Hunter's back.

"Elliot does lots of stuff to help him focus and bring him luck," says Duncan.

I know he's not trying to be mean. But I can tell by the look on Hunter's face that Duncan has just given him something to chew on.

"My dad thinks superstitions are for losers," Hunter says, his teeth bared like a vicious dog. "Only people with no skill believe in them."

"Well, he's wrong." Duncan turns back to his textbook. "We gotta study. See ya, Hunter."

Hunter gives his ball another spin and then strides away. "Later, losers," he calls out.

I try to study, but Hunter's words keep replaying in my head.

Loser. No skill. Jelly.

The numbers on the page swirl around. My right knee bounces up and down under the table.

Duncan looks up. "Dude, you're extra fidgety today. You okay?"

"Just nervous about evaluations, I guess." My excitement over finally being registered for hockey is gone, thanks to Hunter. All I can think about is the coaches up in the bleachers, watching us go through drills. I imagine them picking teams. *Who wants this Elliot kid? He can barely skate.* "I wish we could just skip them and get on with playing. Maybe we *should* skip them. Everyone knows you'll be a one and I'll be a four."

"Evaluations are no big deal."

"Easy for you to say. No one calls *you* Jelly. What would you know about being the worst skater on the ice?"

"Everyone on the team contributes something, Elliot. Not everyone can be the best. Even in the NHL, there are leaders and fighters and goal scorers and…guys who make you laugh in the dressing room—"

"But no one who makes you laugh when they're actually trying to play."

Duncan sighs. "You just need to keep practicing. You need to believe in yourself."

If only it were that simple.

CHAPTER 4

I survive evaluations, and I get put on Coach Matt's team. I'm happy about that until our first practice. The coaches work us so hard, my feet are screaming when I finally take off my skates—hand-me-downs I got from Duncan last year. They're at least a size too small now, but I'm not going to mention that to my parents so soon after they paid the registration fees.

No one else in the dressing room seems as tired as me. Maybe because no one else fell as much as me. So much for this season being better than the last one.

Everyone's talking about some new player who just signed with the Smokies. People here may be die-hard Flames or Canucks fans, but we're all united in our love of the Smoke Eaters. Trail's Junior A hockey team won the Ice Hockey World Championships not once but twice. Everyone still brags about it, even though the last time they won was more than sixty years ago.

While my new teammates argue about whether the Smokies made a good trade, I look around the room, trying to figure out who's who. When we got the email welcoming me to the team, I'd studied the list of names and recognized less than half of them. But at practice today there were more familiar faces on the ice than I'd expected. And a few people from the list that were missing, including the person I was least excited about seeing—Hunter Reid.

Coach Matt throws open the dressing-room door and looks around. "C'mon, guys! Hurry up and get changed! Katherine's waiting to come in. You boys are spending too much time folding your clothes and fixing your hair!"

Jerome Alcot bursts out laughing. "Good one, Coach!"

Jerry's got a voice so loud and deep it sounds like he's talking through a megaphone. He goes to my school, and even though he's a year older, I know him pretty well. Everyone does. We all call him Jerry-Horn.

"But no one calls her Katherine," he adds. "It's Kali."

In hockey, it seems like everyone has a nickname.

"Kali. Right. And it's a good thing we have her." Coach Matt taps his pen against his clipboard. "She's the only one who didn't trip over the blue line out there."

Some of the guys respond by trash-talking back. Coach Matt laughs off their comebacks like a pro. I find the insults hard to take—even when they're not directed at me—but Duncan and his dad are always reminding me that trash talk is part of the game. It means you've been accepted by your team. If they stop trash-talking you, that's when you should worry.

I rush to get out of my sweaty equipment so I'm not the last one to finish. I feel kind of bad for Kali. In U9 and U11, boys and girls share a dressing room. In U13, they split us up.

As the only girl on the team, she's going to miss out on the fun stuff that happens before and after games and practices.

When everyone's decent enough, Kali comes into the dressing room and sits down next to her twin brother, Charlie. Both assistant coaches, Lisa and Tibor, are close behind. Coach Matt talks about his expectations for the season and then goes over the schedule. Last year this all seemed new and exciting. Now I know it's just part of the routine. We don't usually meet after practice—and especially not *after* everyone's changed— but at the first practice of the season, it's different.

While Coach Lisa and Coach Tibor talk about their times playing hockey, I glance around the room to see if anyone else is as impressed as me. They've both played on some really good teams. We're lucky to have them. Coach Tibor especially, since he doesn't even have a kid on the team. It's obvious who

Coach Lisa's son is, though, because she yelled at him a lot when we were on the ice.

"One last thing before we let you go," Coach Matt says after he's answered a bunch of questions. "Does anyone have any experience in net?"

"What? Why?" asks Jerry-Horn. "What's wrong with Hunter?"

"Well, unfortunately, Hunter hurt his knee fooling around on the trampoline." Coach Matt's nose scrunches up. "Not sure how serious it is yet, but he's definitely out for the first month of the season. Maybe longer."

"Can we borrow a goalie from another team? Or call up an AP?" There's a touch of panic in Duncan's voice. Hunter's injury must be very recent if Duncan hasn't talked to his dad about it yet. I don't really like Hunter and was relieved when he didn't show up for practice. But there's no getting around the fact that we need a goalie.

"There's only one goalie on each team this year," says Coach Tibor. "And we can't rely on bringing up someone from U11 because they're short on goalies as well."

"So we're going to play without a goalie?"

Everyone looks at the second-year player who asked this. No one says anything, though. My mind races as I struggle to catch up with what everyone else in the room has probably already figured out. If we can't call up an AP, which Duncan told me stands for *affiliated player*, from U11, what are we going to do? The season hasn't even started yet, and we're already out of the running.

Coach Matt chuckles, then purses his lips. "No one has experience in net, eh? Is anyone interested in trying it out?" He sounds a bit desperate.

Looking down at my sore feet, I get an idea. Maybe, since we have no options, they'd be willing to give *me* a chance to play in goal. Then I wouldn't have to skate as much. And it wouldn't matter that I was always the last one to finish the drills.

I'd still get to play hockey. Plus I'd be an important part of the team.

"I'll do it."

CHAPTER 5

"Are you sure?" Duncan asks me for the zillionth time on the ride home.

"Sure, I'm sure." Truthfully, I'm the exact opposite of sure. Mom and Dad are going to kill me when they find out I volunteered to be goalie. Mom's going to be worried about injuries, and Dad's going to be worried about paying for the equipment necessary to prevent those injuries. I worked so hard to convince my parents to let me play hockey—have I just blown it?

Coach Matt offers to come in and talk to my parents. "Duncan, you stay in the car," he says as he cuts the engine. "This'll only take a sec."

I really, really hope he's right.

"Hi! I'm home!" I announce as I open the front door. This is not something I usually do. I must've seen it in a movie or something.

Only my sister answers. "In here!"

Coach Matt follows me through the empty kitchen and into the den. Aislyn is hunched over her laptop. Several empty water bottles are scattered around her. "Hey, Aislyn."

My sister looks up, surprised. "Oh, hi, Mr. Bilenki!"

"What are you working on?" Coach Matt sounds genuinely interested.

And Aislyn's thrilled to be asked. "I'm trying to figure out how to make an algae bioreactor out of water bottles. It's for the Change Climate Change contest. Did you know that some algae bioreactors can suck as much carbon dioxide out of the atmosphere as an acre of forest? This one won't be that good. But if I can come up with a simple version, everyone could have one. Imagine what a difference it would make!"

Coach Matt whistles. "I only understood about half of what you said, but it sure sounds impressive."

I'm so nervous about telling my parents about the goalie thing that I've twisted the zipper of my jacket around my finger so tight it's cutting off the circulation. "Where's Mom and Dad?"

"Mom's at the farmers market," says Aislyn, "talking to people about her election campaign."

Please let Dad be out too, please let Dad be out too…

"And Dad's in his studio, working on a new carving."

Not good. I have to get out of this mess. "Sorry, Coach Matt. Maybe you should come back later? Dad doesn't like to be bothered when he's working."

"I'm sure Dad won't mind," Aislyn says.

Easy for her to say. Dad never seems to mind when Aislyn interrupts him. But when I do, he always makes me feel bad.

"I hate to bother him, but we need to figure this out now," says Coach Matt. "There's an exhibition game this weekend, which doesn't leave much time for practice."

A boulder as big as the New Jersey Devils Jumbotron settles into my stomach. This is a mistake. Two mistakes. Both of them big.

Mistake number one: asking Dad if I can be goalie.

Mistake number two: me actually being in net, on skates, without much practice.

I take Coach Matt to Dad's studio, walking slower and slower as the boulder settles into my feet. They don't know each other well, but Dad acts happy to see Coach Matt. Until he gets to the part about me volunteering to be goalie.

"What does that mean exactly?" Corkscrew-shaped wood shavings fall from Dad's lumberjack shirt as he squares his shoulders. "Please tell me we don't have to pay more fees."

"No, fees are the same. In some leagues, goalies even get free registration…"

Dad's shoulders relax. Half a smile appears on his face.

"…because their equipment is so expensive."

The smile vanishes.

I stare at the stump Dad's working on. If I squint, I can just make out the crude outline of a bird perched on a log. The bird's wings are spread a little, like he's about to fly away— something I wish I could do right now.

"In this case, I'm pretty sure I can borrow almost everything he needs from the league," Coach Matt continues.

"Almost? Can't he use some of the equipment he's already got? Like his helmet?"

"Some of the undergear will work, but he'll need other stuff, including a proper mask to protect the old noggin." Coach Matt taps a finger against his head.

"Blimey." I can't tell if my dad is mad or just surprised. "The helmet we just bought him last year is top-notch."

"A goalie mask is specifically designed to protect the player not just from impact but from all the pucks that come flying at them."

I was already having doubts about whether I should try to play goal. Now I'm sure—this is a really bad idea.

"If it's a problem, I'll see what I can do. There might be some loaner ones floating around that are the right size. But most goalies have their own equipment at this age."

That's because anyone interested in the position would have been playing goal for at least three years by now. In U9, everyone gets a chance in net. By U11, you're either a goalie or you're not. What was I thinking? My brain must've been in zombie mode when I volunteered for this.

"I think he's okay for now," Coach Matt continues, "but if he sticks with it, you may want to think about getting him some goalie skates, for better ankle protection and mobility."

Even without looking up, I know Dad's burning holes through my skull with his glare. And I can't help thinking about all those pucks flying at me. I cross and uncross my fingers. *Tell him I can't do it*, I urge Dad in my head. *Help me out of this mess.*

Instead Dad thanks Coach Matt and asks him to let us know when he's found the goalie equipment for me. "I'm not bothered by what position he plays, as long as it doesn't cost too much extra."

If there was ever a time for Dad to let me down, this was it. Why did he have to choose now to be supportive?

CHAPTER 6

Coach Matt scores all the equipment for me, as promised, including a goalie mask that smells like a cat peed in it (more than once). I also get an extra-large jersey with the number 1 on the back. I would love to see my last name floating there above the 1. But for some reason U13 teams stop wearing names on the back of their jerseys. In Trail anyway.

Since it took Coach Matt a while to scrape together my goalie gear, I didn't get a chance to practice being in net before the exhibition game. I didn't even get to practice putting on the equipment in the comfort of my own bedroom.

In the dressing room before the game, I struggle to figure out what padding goes where. My teammates are too hyped up to notice how baffled I am. Not that I want them to notice. Sure, I could use the help. It's just that I don't want to give anyone a reason (or another reason) to doubt my ability to pull this off. No one's said anything, but I can sense their fear that something bad's about to happen.

Grandpa once told me he can tell when a storm's coming by the ache in his bones. I don't know exactly what he means, but I think I feel something close to that now.

When the coaches come in for our pre-game talk, I'm not even half-ready. I had the same problem at the beginning of last year. Eventually I figured out a system that worked—jock, leg pads, socks, hockey pants, skates, chest protector, neck guard, elbow pads, jersey, helmet, gloves, stick (always in that order, with the right side first). Apparently, that system doesn't work for goalies. I'm going to have to start over.

Coach Matt turns down the music blaring from Jerry-Horn's speaker. "Okay, team, we've got important stuff to discuss before we take the ice."

The "important stuff" isn't about tactics or attitude or even intel on our opponents. It's about picking a team name. We had talked about it before, and lots of suggestions got bounced around—Hawks, Predators, Destroyers, the usual stuff—but we hadn't picked anything yet.

"How about the Canadiens?" says Charlie.

The more I get to know Kali and Charlie the more different they seem—and not just because Charlie's so much shorter than Kali. I probably shouldn't be surprised. Dad tells everyone that my sister and I are as different as night and day. Except Aislyn and I aren't even biologically related, and Charlie and Kali are twins (something I wouldn't dare say around Kali—she'll clock anyone on the team who refers to them as "the twins").

"I hate names like that!" says Jerry-Horn. "Vancouver *Canucks*, Montreal *Canadiens*, Toronto *Maple Leafs*..." His voice trails off. "It's, like, we get it already, the teams are Canadian! Jeez."

JEROME ALCOT
JERRY-HORN LEFT WING
TRAIL BLAZERS
9

"The Canadiens have way more Stanley Cups than any other team in the league." Charlie wipes his hands down his hockey pants like he's trying to clean them. "They have 24."

"Almost 25," says Duncan. I knew he was talking about their run for the cup that year when all the Canadian teams played in the same division. "Except that was such a short season it probably shouldn't count anyway."

Charlie nods. "Even with 24 they're far ahead of everyone else. The Leafs have the second most wins with 13. I don't think it's such a bad thing to be Canadian. Or Canadien."

This guy sure knows his stats. Even though I'm not allowed to watch much hockey, I'm pretty good with my NHL facts—mostly because of all the books Grandpa's sent me—but Charlie is like a walking Wikipedia page.

"Good suggestions, everyone." Coach Matt claps. "Let's focus. Time to vote. We've got to get on the ice."

I glance at the goalie pads lying on the floor in front of me. Panic ricochets through my veins, and I wonder if Grandpa's ever felt this jittery.

"How about the Blazers?" Kali suggests.

"Trail Blazers," says Coach Lisa. "Blazers. I like it."

"What's a trailblazer?" asks one of the second-year players whose name I've finally figured out. He punctuates the question with a fart.

LOGAN LUFT
TRAIL BLAZERS   CENTER

FARTSBY

28

28

Laughter fills the dressing room. Logan is known for this particular talent—and the smells that come with it.

"It's an expression, Fartsby," says Duncan. It's no secret that Logan's favorite player is Sidney Crosby—he wears a Crosby jersey to every practice and a Penguins cap with "Sid the Kid" written on the brim whenever he's not on the ice. That only explains half the nickname, though. He'd clearly earned the other half with his own talent. He didn't seem to mind it though. "You know, like, 'he was such a trailblazer'?"

"Or 'she,'" adds Kali.

"And don't forget the Portland Trail Blazers, who made it to the playoffs twenty-one years in a row, from 1983 through 2003." Apparently Charlie's got the NBA covered too.

"Enough chatter," says Jerry-Horn. "Let's just go with the Blazers so we can get this party started." He stands up like it's a done deal.

"All in favor?" asks Coach Matt.

It's unanimous. Or close enough. I don't bother counting hands as I tug at the new-to-me neck guard strangling me to death.

"Elliot, Coach Tibor's going to stay behind to help you finish getting your gear on," Coach Matt says as the rest of the team files out. "We can start warm-up without a goalie. Plus it's good to keep the other team in suspense."

I'm sure everyone's in suspense, not just the other team, waiting to see how I'll do—including me. When we play street hockey or mini sticks, I'm pretty good in net. But as Duncan keeps telling me, there's a big difference between goaltending on ice and goaltending on pavement.

"Can you do up your skates?" Coach Tibor's voice echoes off the cement walls of the now-empty dressing room. I'd always thought it was nice of Coach Tibor to volunteer when he doesn't even have kids. Since he started telling us stories about when he played for a team in the Czech Republic, I'm even more grateful. Especially since he was a goalie, and we need all the help we can get in that department.

TIBOR WALLACE
SPARTA PRAHA   GOALIE

"Yep. I can tie my own skates." Mom bought me waxed laces when she heard that coaches don't help kids with their skates in U13. Not that I need them. My skates are so small they're tight enough before I even tie them up.

When I'm done, Coach Tibor strings my skates with extra lace and tells me to lie down on my stomach so he can help strap on my goalie pads. It's a relief to have someone who knows what they're doing talk me through it. I'm just glad my teammates can't see me in this position.

"All you have to do is stay on your feet," Coach Tibor says as he clips on the various straps. "Everyone's going to be rusty after a whole summer off the ice. Stand strong and you'll be fine."

"Stand strong" sounds like good advice, but I need help just getting up off the floor. When Coach Tibor finally has me seated on the bench, he tugs the number 1 jersey over my head.

The rough fabric stretches across layers of padding, and suddenly extra-large doesn't seem so big anymore.

Next comes the mask, which I can't put on myself because my chest protector and arm pads are so stiff I can barely move. How am I going to stop the puck if I can't move my arms?

"This mask is a bit big for you. But I've adjusted it as much as I can," Coach Tibor says after fiddling with the skull and chin straps for a while.

"It's okay," I say quickly. It feels like my teammates have been out on the ice forever. If I'm going to do this, I better do it now. Before I totally lose my nerve.

"I think you're ready," Coach Tibor announces, doing one final check to make sure there's nothing left in the bag of borrowed equipment.

For one heart-stopping second I think I forgot my cup. But then I realize I put it on so long ago it might as well have been yesterday. "Thanks for your help. I'm never going to be able to do this on my own," I say.

"You'll get used to it," Coach Tibor assures me.

I walk out of the dressing room, certain I am going to fall on my face at any moment. But I don't. Because Coach Tibor is next to me, keeping me steady. "You got this," he says as he opens the gate and pats me on the head.

My mask slumps so far forward I can't see through the cage. Mom's going to freak when she sees how big it is—*if* she sees how big it is. She promised she'd be cheering me on from the stands. But she's been very distracted lately.

I push my mask back into place. "I've got this," I mutter. And for a moment, I really think I do. I take a deep breath and step out onto the ice.

And fall flat on my face.

CHAPTER 7

"We lost! No, we didn't just lose. We got *crushed*!"

"I know. I was there." Mom hands me a banana.

I take it. But only because bananas are my favorite food. "Just for the first period."

"Sorry, hon. I had to take Aislyn to an event at the maker space." She glances at her watch. Aislyn's still there and needs a ride home. Which means Mom had time to drop her off and come back to the game. But she didn't.

"It doesn't matter," I mumble. "The second and third periods were much, much worse. I don't even know the final score because the referees made them stop adding the other team's goals to the scoreboard. I didn't stop a single shot. I couldn't even move without falling. And once I was down, I couldn't get back up!"

"Don't be so hard on yourself." Mom's calm-down voice, meant to be soothing, sounds like sandpaper on metal to my ears.

I peel the banana and shove it in my face. Mouth full, I try to say more, but the words come out as a jumbled mess. I skip from one horror story to the next—how embarrassing it was (a thousand times worse than the time I accidentally went into the girls' bathroom in third grade), how the game seemed to go on forever (and ever) and how little my teammates talked to me afterward (not even trash talk).

I swallow. Hard. A big lump of banana gets lodged in my throat.

"It was your first time in net," says Mom.

"Also my last. I'm not playing in goal ever again."

"Don't talk rubbish," says my dad. "You made a commitment to Coach Matt. And the team. You can't just quit."

I look up to see Dad standing there, his work pants covered in wood dust. I was already out of breath. Now I'm suffocating. "Yes, I can. Right, Mom?"

Mom glances back and forth between Dad and me a couple of times as I put my hands behind my back. I've crossed and uncrossed my fingers nine times when she finally answers. "The Feldner-Martels aren't quitters—"

There's no time to count to ten, take a deep breath or do any of the tricks I've been taught to calm me down. I hurl my banana peel at the sink. It makes a splat on the wall that does nothing to ease the storm raging inside me. "I never said I was quitting! I just said I wasn't going to be goalie!"

"Calm down," Dad orders in a voice that's the exact opposite of calm. "Throwing things is not an acceptable way of dealing with your frustration. How old are you? Three?"

"You're such a jerk! Mom and I were talking. No one asked you to butt in—"

"Don't speak to your father that way, Elliot."

"One more word and you'll be out of hockey for good, E," Dad snaps.

I can't quit being goalie but Dad can make me quit the team? The molten lava smoldering inside me erupts. I yank the baseball cap off my head. I'm about to throw it when Mom puts her hand on my shoulder and steers me toward the staircase.

"Why don't you go take a shower," Mom says. "We'll talk about this later, when everyone's calmed down."

I really want to kick the banister. I force myself not to, knowing it will only make things worse. And I really don't want to make things worse. Especially for Mom, who always has to work so hard to keep Dad and me from blowing up.

1, Calgary Flames, 2, Edmonton Oilers, 3, Vancouver Canucks, 4, Winnipeg Jets, 5, Ottawa Senators…

Clenching my fists, I take the stairs two at a time.

Replays of every goal I let in run through my head as I shower. Eventually I feel my shoulders start to relax, and my mind drifts to Dad and why I let him get to me so much.

Mom says I've always gotten upset easily. She took me to a doctor to talk about it once. The doctor made me answer a bunch of questions and ordered some tests to look at my brain.

I'll never forget how relieved I felt when the doctor told my parents there was nothing wrong with me. Speaking directly to me, she said that all kids deal with emotions differently and that it is okay to feel big things. Still, that's when Mom started buying tons of books about emotional regulation and anxiety management. She also taught me to count things to help me calm down.

By the time I get out of the shower, my skin's wrinkled and I'm sorry for how I acted. I know I have to apologize, but sometimes I wish Dad would apologize too. I'm not the only one in our family who gets mad.

Back in my room I pull on a pair of sweats. There's a knock at the door. When I open it, Aislyn's hovering in the hallway, holding the laptop and looking nervous. Now I feel even worse.

I bet Mom warned her that I was upset about the game. Sometimes when I'm mad—and especially when Dad and I fight—I take it out on her. I'm getting better, but Mom still tries to keep Aislyn away from me when she thinks I might snap at her.

"Grandpa's on the computer," she says. "He wants to talk to you."

"Thanks," I say, taking the laptop from her. I add a smile, hoping she knows that means I'm okay, and close the door.

I sit down at my desk and open the computer. Grandpa grins at me on the screen. It's good to see him looking so happy. He's been having a bunch of medical tests lately. And last time we talked, he looked a bit green. I blamed it on Aislyn playing with the picture settings, but truthfully, it worried me.

"Heard you had a tough game, Sport," he says.

I tell him about it in much more detail—and with much less anger—than I managed with Mom. Besides me, Grandpa's the only one in the family who likes hockey. He played a few seasons for the Dolbeau Castors in the Saguenay Lac St-Jean Senior League. Even though I'm sure Grandpa has never stunk as bad as I did on the ice today, talking to him makes me feel a little better.

"You're not going to like this, Sport, but I think your parents are right," Grandpa says when I'm done. "You should give it another shot."

The better feeling disappears. I wish they hadn't been talking behind my back. Telling Aislyn about the fight is one thing. Telling Grandpa about it is another.

Twisting an elastic band around my finger, I try to stay *grounded*.

Grandpa moves his face closer to the screen, so close I can see his nostril hairs. "I heard you need a new goalie mask. I'm going to order one for you. I'll pay extra for shipping so it gets there in time for your next game."

Oh no. I'm grateful that he is being so generous. But if I accept this gift, I'll have to stay in net.

Ignoring my protests, Grandpa keeps talking. "With a little luck, it'll even be there for your next practice. It's not safe to be playing with a mask that doesn't fit properly. I can't believe they put you out there like that. Without any practice."

Snap! The elastic flies off my finger and across the room. Mom must've told him the loaner mask was too big. Did everyone else notice it too? And how much I struggled to see through the cage?

Maybe Grandpa's right. Maybe the loss wasn't all my fault. Without me, the Trail Blazers wouldn't have had a goalie at all. If I quit, we'll have to default our first game of the season. Nothing great about that. "But what if my second game's as bad as my first?" I ask.

"It won't be," says Grandpa confidently. "Because you'll have time to practice. And you'll have a mask that actually fits."

"I guess. Thanks, Grandpa."

"Did you like that book I sent you? I bet Carey Price has some good tips and tricks."

The book is called *How a First Nations Kid Became a Superstar Goaltender.* I loved reading about how Carey's dad built him a rink on the creek behind their house when Carey was only two. And how, when he was nine, his dad flew him to hockey games—in a plane described as a trash can with wings—because they lived too far away to drive to them. Now Carey is the goalie with the most wins in Montreal Canadiens history. How can a scrawny kid like me, who can barely skate, even dream of being a superstar like him?

After saying goodbye to Grandpa, I run my fingers over my collection of bobbleheads. I pick up the Carey Price one. Grandpa sent it to me so long ago that the paint on its blue jersey is starting to fade. "Could you really help me?" I ask.

The head bobbles back. It almost looks like it's nodding.

"Okay then…just give me one win," I whisper. "Or at least a tie. That's all I ask."

I give it another little shake so it has no choice but to agree.

CHAPTER 8

The mask doesn't arrive in time for Wednesday's practice—which is brutal. I thought practice was tough before. As goalie, it's eight hundred million times worse. I'm not exaggerating.

I wish I could say it's because I was stuck wearing gear that doesn't fit. But that's not the only reason.

During warm-up, goalies have to skate with everyone else. Skating was already hard for me, and now I have to do it wearing a hundred pounds of extra equipment. The only good thing about it is that at least I have an excuse for being the slowest.

Once practice starts, I get shot at over and over and over again with no breaks. Instead of one puck on the ice, there's millions. My teammates don't wait for me to recover from my last save (or save *attempt*) before firing at me again. And when they score? They pump their arms in the air like they've just beaten a Vezina Trophy winner and not me—their rookie goalie who was looking the other way because someone else was shooting at them at the *same time*.

Coach Matt must sense how miserable I am, because in the dressing room after practice he starts by telling me that if Saturday's game doesn't go well, I don't have to stay in net. Some pep talk.

A hush settles over the dressing room. My face—already redder than a Flames jersey from all the huffing and puffing I did during practice—ignites. I know everyone's waiting to see how I will respond. They're all counting on me. I want so desperately to help my team, I can taste it.

Logan lets one rip, and the spell's broken.

Jerry-Horn waves a hand in front of his nose. "Maybe you should lay off the egg-salad sandwiches, Fartsby."

Fartsby laughs, and fart jokes fly around the room. Coach Matt's comment about me not staying in net is forgotten.

I guess I don't need to say anything about the next game. I just need to show up.

It doesn't take long for me to get ready for our first game of the season. At least, not compared to how long it took me to get ready for the exhibition game. I've practiced putting on my gear at home so many times that I'm even starting to develop a routine, one that already feels luckier than last season's. Plus my new mask—which arrived on Thursday and smells like Coach Matt's car after he's cleaned it—fits perfectly.

I wish I could say the same about my skates. My toes are jammed so hard against the end I'm worried they might actually break.

I'm not as far behind my teammates getting on the ice either, something I actually manage to do without falling.

Not falling's good—obviously—but being on the ice earlier is not. More time on the ice before the game starts means more shots flying past my head and more pucks sliding into the net behind me.

When Coach Matt calls us over for the pre-game huddle, I'm already exhausted. And frustrated.

Kali looks up at the score clock. "Are we home or away?"

Fartsby frowns. "Home. Duh. We're in Trail."

"Both teams are from Trail." Jerry-Horn laughs. "This is the home arena for the Rebels and the Blazers."

I try to concentrate on the pre-game banter, but I'm distracted by the other team. The Rebels players suddenly seem so big. Their goalie's at least twice as wide as me, I swear.

"Okay, Blazers. Listen up." Coach Lisa stands on the bench and shouts to be heard over everyone's chatter. "Coach Tibor's organizing D, and I'm on O. But here's the thing. Defense is top priority in this game. I don't want to see any risk-taking from my forwards. No risks. We are protecting our goalie in this game. Protect the goalie—that's top priority."

Gulp. As if I wasn't feeling bad enough already. Goalies aren't supposed to be protected. They're supposed to be the protector—of the net anyway.

The ref blows the whistle.

"Remember all the things we worked on in practice." Coach Tibor pushes me away from the bench like I'm riding a bike for the first time. If only skates came with training wheels.

"You got this," he says.

I feel like everyone's watching as I skate over to the net and try to rough up the crease like I've seen Carey Price do in the replays.

Problem is, I can't do a proper hockey stop, so instead of actually roughing up the ice, I just glide awkwardly from side to side.

Fartsby takes the face-off and wins. Jerry-Horn carries the puck into the Rebels zone. When their goalie commits, he chips the puck to Charlie in the slot.

The goalie kicks aside Charlie's attempt at a tip-in. Fartsby picks up the rebound and passes it to Duncan at the point. Duncan winds up for the shot…

…and fans on it.

The Rebels regain the puck and break out of the zone for a two-on-one. They pass back and forth. Tic-tac-toe. This is Duncan's and his cousins' favorite street-hockey move. I glide over to block on *toe*, angling toward the guy I bet will shoot. Pushing my pad against the net, I go down on one knee and hope for the best.

The puck hits my shoulder, knocking me off-balance. I lose sight of it for a moment. But as I fall backward, I spot the puck in the crease. I drop my blocker on top of it.

The referee blows the whistle, and the linesman skates over. My hands are shaking so hard I can't move my blocker to hand it to him.

I just made a save. And covered up the rebound.

Maybe this goalie thing isn't so bad after all.

CHAPTER 9

"Nice work, Jelly!" Kali taps her stick against my pads before lining up for the face-off. The crossbar digs into my back as I lean against the net for support.

"Sorry I left you short, Elliot." Duncan grabs my cage, pulling me forward enough that I almost fall again. Even Duncan's forgetting how unsteady I am on skates. "That was a great save."

It's not the last.

At the end of the first period, it's 2–2.

At the end of the second, it's 5–5.

Every time we score, the Rebels answer back. When we're tied, it's like I'm standing on my head—nothing gets past me no matter how much I flop around on the ice. But when we take the lead, the Rebels' next shot almost always goes in.

The game stays knotted at 6 for the entire third period. Everyone seems to be getting tired, so the shots aren't as hard. Still, I'm making saves I never thought I could make.

With two minutes left, Maddox "Madder" Carter poke-checks the puck away from a Rebels defenseman at the blue line.

It's a risky play, but it pays off. Madder gobbles up the loose puck and charges out of the zone for a breakaway. Nobody on either team has a hope of catching him as he rushes toward the Rebels' net. When he hits the hash marks, Madder toe-drags before unleashing a shot that sneaks through the five-hole.

SCORE!

Madder does the eagle—lifting one skate off the ice and flapping his arms—as he glides away from the net. The Blazers on the ice meet him in the neutral zone, circling him in celebration.

We're ahead 7–6. Standing alone, I glance at the clock. Thirty-four seconds left.

When I'm playing *NHL All-Stars*, half a minute goes by faster than Connor McDavid in a skating competition. But at the end of a real game—when the losing team pulls its goalie and six players start desperately firing shots at the winning team's net—each hundredth of a second feels like an eternity. Can I keep the puck out of the net long enough to get my first win?

"Time-out for the Blazers!" yells the ref.

Everyone gathers around Coach Matt at the bench. I hobble toward them, my skates threatening to burst apart with every stride.

Aiming for an open spot at the end of the bench, I reach forward to try to stop myself by grabbing on to the boards. But when my blocker makes contact, I ricochet back like a marble in a pinball machine.

Madder grabs my elbow and pulls me into the huddle.

"Thanks." I smile. "And great goal, Madder. Loved the celly!"

"Ease up on the showboating," Coach Lisa says to her son. "It just gets the other team riled up against us. Remember?"

I squirt water into my mouth and try to focus as Coach Matt explains the game plan—do whatever it takes to keep the puck out of our end, even if it means taking a penalty. No one looks at me, but I can tell they're all thinking what I'm thinking. *If only Hunter were in net instead of Elliot.*

"You kept them in the game," Coach Tibor says to me when the whistle blows. "Now help your team finish it off."

I skate toward the net, hoping for two things:

1. I don't fall before the play even starts.
2. We win the face-off.

The first one happens. The second one doesn't.

With the Rebels in control of the puck, their goalie skates to the bench and another player comes on. Four forwards cross center line. I try to make myself look as big as I can even though I feel as small and useless as belly-button lint.

The Rebels storm the net. I block a shot from the winger. The rebound immediately gets away from me.

Their center takes another shot. And another. He's hammering at the puck, which is somewhere in front of my pads.

Blow the whistle, ref!

No whistle.

A different Rebel player whacks my skate. The puck jumps out of the crease. Just as I'm about to lose balance, I dive forward. I pull my arms and legs into my body like I'm making a snow angel, certain the puck's under my stomach somewhere. The ref has to blow the whistle now—I've got it covered.

But there's no whistle. Instead it's the horn.

Game over.

We won!

I float through the handshakes and don't come back to earth until we're back in the dressing room.

"Way to use your belly, Jelly!"

"It's about time those wobbly legs of yours did some good."

"Were you trying to stop that puck or did you just accidentally get in the way?"

For the first time ever, being trash-talked by my teammates doesn't sting. It feels like acceptance.

"So we have a goalie until Hunter comes back?" Coach Matt asks.

Everyone's looking at me.

"You bet," I reply.

CHAPTER 10

On Sunday I get into one of what Mom likes to call my stormy moods.

I don't know why I am so irritable. Maybe it's because Mom and Aislyn don't want to hear any more about my game-ending save. Not that I can blame them. I've talked about it constantly while doing more than a couple slo-mo replays.

I think what's really bugging me is knowing that I got the win without having a clue what I was doing. Now my teammates are going to expect me to do it again—and I don't know if I can.

I don't get my English project done, which makes for a miserable Monday morning as well. But when Jerry-Horn waves Duncan and me over to his lunch table, the cloud hanging over me finally starts to lift.

I know it sounds silly, but for me, having lunch with the other hockey players is one of the highlights of being on the team. In past years Duncan would invite me to sit with them, but I never felt like I really belonged. So we'd sit slightly apart from them instead—an in-between place where neither of us belonged.

Now we're at a table surrounded by Blazers. All eyes are on Jerry-Horn as he does a re-enactment of his own. He's already into the final minutes of the third period. His description of Madder's breakaway is different than the way I remember it. Especially the part about Jerry-Horn taking out the other team's defensive player so he couldn't back-check Madder.

Duncan slides his tray down the table a little, like he's trying to put some distance between himself and Jerry-Horn. His sandwich looks way yummier than my leftover white-bean and kale quesadillas, but, like me, he hasn't eaten much.

"I think your mom would've killed you if you hadn't scored that goal," says Dyne. He's sitting across from me. In front of him is a tray so packed with food it's spilling over the sides.

"If I hadn't scored, someone else would have." Madder shrugs. "But Mom and I did talk about it on the way home."

Kali fakes a shiver that makes the whole table shake. "Your mom's tough stuff."

"She's just super competitive." Madder runs his fingers through his thick black hair. "We review most of the game afterward. It really helps." He's not the biggest kid on our team, but he's one of the best. I like the way he can always read the play. Did his mom teach him that? Or is it a talent he was born with?

Nibbling at a dry bit of tortilla, I wait for Jerry-Horn to finish his story.

"Thirty-four seconds left. And all the pressure lies on the shoulders of this man." Jerry-Horn, in full performance mode, points to me with both hands. "Our new goalie."

"Jelly-Legs!" Crumbs fly from Dyne's mouth.

Jerry-Horn carries on, and once again I'm surprised by the details he adds. How our defense was trying to take down the Rebels in front of the net. How our offense had collapsed in to try to clear away the rebound. How our coaches were going nuts on the bench.

Last season I always felt like I was on the outside looking in—even when I was on the ice. But on Saturday I had been on the inside, so busy making the save that I hadn't even had time to look out. Is this what it's like to be truly part of a team?

I give up on the quesadilla and peel my banana as I lean into the story. Jerry-Horn's right at the best part. "Then suddenly, like a tree being chopped down, Elliot 'Jelly-Legs' Feldner-Martel falls forward." He makes a chopping motion with his hand. "TIMBER! Right onto the puck. WHAT A SAVE!"

People sitting around us turn to look. "I'm talking about this guy." Jerry-Horn points to me again, his fingers and thumbs in the shape of a gun. "Hero of the game."

Warmth rushes through me. I'm embarrassed. But I'm not.

Beside me Duncan tenses. There are people at our school—at the next table, actually—who play on the other Trail teams, including the Rebels. Some of them were Duncan's teammates before, and he considers them friends. Bragging about a win is not what Duncan considers good sportsmanship.

Over the regular cafeteria racket—people talking, forks scraping, trays banging—I hear a loud metallic *thunk* as a pair of crutches hits the table next to me.

Instead of greeting everyone at the table, Hunter directs his eyes at me like he's lining me up in the scope of a gun. "You eat a lot of bananas, Jelly. Are you part monkey or something?"

I drop my banana as if I've just discovered it's covered in maggots.

"That would explain how you play in net," he continues. "You go down on your knees way too soon."

"But not your belly." Dyne nods at me. "The timing of that belly flop was just right."

I respond with a weak smile, grateful to him for cutting Hunter off. But even with Dyne's support, I'm suddenly right back where I was last year—on the outside looking in.

Pushing away from the table, I watch as Jerry-Horn moves Hunter's crutches to the side and helps him sit down. "How come you weren't on the bench with us on Saturday, dude?"

"We got to the arena after the game started," Hunter replies. "Mom booked another appointment because she didn't think I needed to be there. Dad went berserk. I'll be on the bench for all the games from now on."

"Won't that be boring?" asks Fartsby. "Being on the bench and not being able to play?"

"No doubt," agrees Kali. "As boring as watching Canada destroy a team like Italy in the World Junior Championship."

"Dad says I have to stay with my team so I'm ready to play." Hunter's taking up way too much room as he unwraps his sandwich. "He doesn't understand how Jelly managed to get a win when he can't even skate."

"Coach Matt says I have good hands," I mutter, my heart suddenly beating so fast I can feel it pulsing in my throat.

Hunter smirks. "Do your hands fall off when you get to practice?"

Heat flares across my face. I want to punch a hole through the brick wall next to us and stuff Hunter inside. My eyes scan the table as I try to ground myself the way my mom taught me.

1, apple sauce, 2, chocolate milk, 3, yogurt, 4, granola bar...

As I start to see what everyone's eating, I also start noticing the different smells—including some that are actually good, like Dyne's vanilla pudding. The seat beneath me feels strong and steady. My heart rate begins to slow.

"When will you be back on the ice?" Duncan asks Hunter.

Instead of answering, Hunter says a bunch of stuff about surgery, physio and needing an MRI to figure it all out. Everyone nods like they totally understand. Not me. ACL, MRI...I worked hard to figure out all the hockey acronyms last season. Now I have to learn more. Thanks to Hunter.

Then again, I also have Hunter to thank for giving me a chance to find my place on the team. Goalie's my ticket to fitting in. I'm sure of it. And I never would've gotten here—not just to this lunch table but to the center of Jerry-Horn's play-by-play—if it hadn't been for Hunter's injured BLT (or whatever that ligament in his knee's called).

Grandpa needed an MRI recently. But he had to wait a long time for the appointment. So I'm guessing Hunter will have to wait a while too. In the meantime, why can't I enjoy being a part of things?

I realize I am famished. I attack my quesadillas like they're potato chips. "Hopefully you come back soon," I say between bites.

Just not too soon…

CHAPTER 11

The Blazers practice twice a week. On Tuesdays we're on the kids' rink, so we get the ice to ourselves. Wednesdays, we share the big ice with another Trail team.

In both practices I'm terrible. But on Wednesday I'm even worse than terrible. In fact, I'm so bad during a scrimmage between the two teams that Coach Tibor comes out on the ice to stand next to me and give me pointers. Without any equipment on—just skates, a helmet and a stick—he makes more saves than I do. It's not even close.

On the way home I sit in the back of Coach Matt's car with my arms crossed and my head down. I haven't showered yet, so I can smell my stink. In a weird way it's comforting.

"Remember, a lot of the game is mental," Coach Matt says as he pulls into my driveway. "Don't let one bad practice get into your head, eh? Start visualizing how great you're going to play on Sunday."

I haul my hockey bag out of the trunk. "Thanks, Coach. See you tomorrow, Duncan."

"See ya, Jell—" Duncan stops short. "I mean, Elliot."

I'm not mad at Duncan for almost using the nickname. I get it. No one calls Duncan Can Can off the ice, but during hockey season I hear it so much that I sometimes have to think before I call him anything at all.

Still, it makes me wonder if the way I feel about the nickname has changed. Am I the Jelly my teammates made fun of last season because my legs were so wobbly? Or the star of Jerry-Horn's story for my strong, game-winning save?

Sinking into the den couch, I think about my Carey Price bobblehead and what I said to it after talking to Grandpa. Is it just a coincidence that I asked for a win and then got one? It must be—I might be superstitious, but it's not like I believe in magic.

Stretching out my legs, I dig into a bag of mini sour-cream-and-onion rice chips. My foot hits the end of the couch. Pain ricochets up my leg.

I peel off my socks to investigate. Blisters cover not just the back but the sides of both feet as well.

My skates!

The blisters must've formed on Saturday. I guess I was so thrilled with the win, I didn't even notice. But at practice the blisters were preventing me from moving as well as I did in the game.

It makes so much sense now. I can't believe I didn't figure it out earlier. Somehow I have to get new skates. As soon as possible. Or my days as a goalie are over.

Everyone's in different corners of the house—Mom in her office, Dad in his studio, Aislyn in her room. I use the silence to prepare. First I hang my damp hockey equipment in the garage the way Dad's always nagging me to do. Then I take a shower so Mom doesn't have to remind me. I even put my sweaty clothes in the washing machine. And turn it on.

Next I start getting things out for dinner. When Dad's having a "studio day," he usually gets the evening meal prepared in the morning so he doesn't have to stop working right when "the juices are flowing." (I have no idea what he means by that).

Sure enough, there's a pot of something in the fridge. I put it on the stove and slice the loaf of multigrain bread on the counter. I'm about to set the table when Mom comes into the kitchen.

"What smells so good?"

I take a sniff of the peppery broth bubbling in the pot. "Stew maybe? Dad made it. I'm just helping to get dinner on the table."

"That's amazing, honey." Mom gets cups while I set out the cutlery. "Thank you so much. It's been a long day."

"But it's over now, right?"

"I have more work to do after dinner, unfortunately." Mom pours herself a glass of wine—something she never does on weekdays—and slides onto one of the stools. "This campaign's a lot more than I bargained for."

"Lots of people think you'd make a great mayor," I say as I grab the butter from the fridge. "I bet you'd get elected without doing anything at all."

Mom laughs. "I'm not sure it works that way. But thanks for the vote of confidence. How was your day?"

"Okay. But hockey practice was tough. And I think I might need new skates." I hold up one of my feet for her to see. After my shower, the blisters look even more alarming.

"Oh my gosh!" Mom exclaims. "Why didn't you tell me about this earlier?"

"Sorry. I knew my skates were too small, but I didn't know about the blisters until today. I thought I could tough it out. With registration fees, I thought it might be too much if I asked for new equipment too."

"Oh, honey, you should've told us. We'll figure something out. But first let's get these feet bandaged properly so you don't do any more damage."

"Dad's going to be mad. He already thinks hockey's too expensive."

Mom takes a sip of wine. "Well, I did max out our credit card with election signs and brochures. So we can't buy you new skates until next month. But maybe there's a way you can earn the money yourself."

I was not expecting this conversation to go so well. And I like the idea of buying my own skates. "Yes! I could mow lawns or shovel snow."

"I was also thinking you could help me hand out flyers and put up signs."

"Isn't that more of an Aislyn thing?"

"Aislyn doesn't believe in cutting down trees to make printed materials. She's helping with my website instead."

"But you just said you can't afford to pay me. How will that help me earn money for new skates?"

"If you come with me as I do my door-to-door visits, you can introduce yourself and ask if anyone needs anything done around their place."

"That's a great idea," I say. "Thanks, Mom."

It all sounds like a lot of work. But I want new skates as soon as possible. I *need* new skates. And maybe—if I work hard enough—I can even get goalie skates. Duncan says they cost a bit more, but they're lower on the ankle so you can move your feet better. Plus they give you more protection.

If I'm going to keep doing this goalie thing, I need every advantage—and all the protection—I can get.

CHAPTER 12

Before our game against the Nelson Leafs on Sunday, Mom bandages my feet with moleskin and tape. She also replaces the insoles, gives me a thinner pair of socks and re-laces my skates—all hacks she found on YouTube.

Once my skates are on, I barely even feel the blisters. This is good, especially since it's looking like new skates are not in my immediate future. I struck out with almost all my neighbors on getting work. Turns out the end of October's a horrible time to earn money mowing grass (because it's not growing anymore) or shoveling snow (because it's not falling yet). I got one job raking leaves and that's it.

I sit in my regular spot as I wait for Kali and the coaches to arrive, going through the pre-game routine in my head to make sure I didn't miss anything. Grayson Lampert's sitting next to me. He's fast on the ice but slow in the dressing room and is only half-ready to go.

As he pulls out his socks, a horrible stink fills the dressing room. It's so strong there's almost a shape to it—a sick green blob that hovers over us like something from a comic book.

"Eww!" Kali enters the room, waving a hand in front of her nose. "What's that gross smell?"

"Is it your socks, Gray?" asks Charlie.

Gray nods proudly and waves his socks in the air, fanning the fumes so much that I'm sure the team in the next dressing room can smell them. "My lucky socks never get washed!"

"He did it last year too," Charlie says. "By the end of the season his socks pretty much stood on their own."

Everyone laughs. Then Hunter says, "Superstitions are for sissies."

I'm holding my breath, waiting—hoping—for someone to disagree.

"Yeah, superstitions suck," says Dyne. "That's little-kid stuff."

"Time to grow up!" Jerry-Horn agrees. "And get your mom to wash your socks."

Kali's long brown braid swings defiantly across her back. "Or do it yourself!"

Gray laughs and grabs a Halloween candy from the bag Dyne's mom gave him to share with the team. He clearly doesn't care what people think.

I try not to either. But I'm bummed that some of my teammates feel the same way about superstitions as Hunter does. What would they say if they found out I had a chat with my Carey Price bobblehead before coming to the game? I didn't make another wish—not exactly—but I figured it didn't hurt to add a pre-game pep talk to my list of rituals.

As everyone continues to joke about superstitions, I feel worse and worse. Counting never stops the hurt—just the anger—so I crawl inside my head and think about how much fun Duncan and I had trick-or-treating this year.

We went in the same Mario and Luigi costumes we wore last year. The shirts were a bit tight, but the hats fit. Aislyn—wearing a yellow mustache and eyebrows that sort of made her look like the Lorax—went from house to house yelling "trick or *tree*." Instead of asking for treats, she asked for donations to one of her favorite environmental groups. It was annoying but also kind of cool (except that she's now stealing candy from the small stash Dad let me keep).

As Coach Tibor tightens my leg pads, I realize I haven't heard anything the coaches said during the pep talk. But I'm feeling calm. While we wait for the officials to open the gate, I also realize that thinking about Halloween stopped me from getting too nervous.

Pretty much the entire first period's played at the Leafs' end of the ice. At first I'm relieved. Then I start getting bored because there's nothing for me to do. Under all this equipment, I'm actually getting a bit cold. And I have to pee.

With two minutes left I whack my stick against the ice. I've seen other goalies do this when the play's in the other zone. I'm not sure why. It warms me up a bit, but I'm guessing the pros do it to distract the other team. Or maybe it's a dare, their way of saying, *Bring it on.*

Sure enough, the next play is a three-on-two rush in my direction. Coach Tibor yells at me to come farther out of the net. I want to, but I'm afraid I'll fall.

The Leafs center gets in really close. I back up a bit before dropping into a butterfly.

He passes to the left wing. I can't slide over, and I can't get back up.

I'm in full panic mode as the winger shoots a wrister over my shoulder. I see it coming all the way, but it's as if my goalie stick has anchored me to the ice. I can't get my blocker up in time.

Not even close.

The Leaf's arms fly up in victory as I sink down in defeat. With just one shot, the Leafs are on the board.

The Blazers answer back. More than once. At the end of the first period, we're up 5–1. The Leafs still have only one shot on net.

"You've got to keep your head up," Coach Lisa tells Madder when we skate in for the two-minute break between periods. "Head up! Don't get sloppy just because they aren't giving us much competition."

I look over at Coach Tibor to see if he has any advice for me. He just smiles. I'm not surprised—Coach Tibor likes to focus on the good, and I haven't done anything but let in a goal.

"Okay, team, I want to see some good sportsmanship out there. We don't need to run up the score too much," Coach Matt says. "I want to see everyone pass at least once before taking a shot. This is a chance to focus on teamwork."

Holding on to the boards, I shuffle back and forth, trying to ignore the pressure on my bladder as I listen to the rest of Coach Matt's speech. If only there were enough time to use the bathroom. I can't even get to the dressing room in two minutes—there's no way I could strip off enough gear to get the job done.

The rest of the game's pretty much the same as the first period. The Leafs defense is so weak that we're able to get in deep with lots of shots, even after passing it around like Coach Matt instructed. Their goalie's decent, except that he gives up a lot of rebounds, which we gobble up like hungry hyenas.

Coach Lisa doesn't stop yelling—I don't think she can stop herself from pointing out how her players can improve—but everyone else is pretty quiet, even the parents. Defensive part-ners get switched and forward lines get mixed to keep things interesting. But even with the changes, Fartsby gets a hat trick, and Charlie—who's not a big goal scorer—pockets one as well.

I try my best but still let in almost every shot the Leafs take, which is luckily not many. It helps that our defense is strong. Kali makes a play that should be on the NHL highlight reel when she dives to poke-check the puck off the stick of a Leaf about to go on a breakaway. The game ends 13–9 Blazers.

"You sure made them work hard out there, Jelly," Hunter says in the dressing room afterward. "Not! That should've been a total shutout."

"My skates are too tight," I mumble. "Plus I had to pee."

Hunter goes on like he didn't hear me. He's already in his street clothes, so there's nothing for him to do but trash-talk. Blazers who didn't score are losers. Blazers who did score are puck hogs. The only person who did nothing wrong was Hunter himself, because how hard can it be to sit on the bench? I tug at my straps and say nothing as Hunter imitates one of the goals I let in.

"We get it," says Duncan.

"Really, Can Can?" Hunter pauses in mid-motion. "That's quick for you."

"Harsh." Rashid, who everyone calls Seven because that's the number he always gets, rubs his hands together. He's only just become a Trail Blazer—he was in the United Arab Emirates visiting family when the season started—but I like him already. "Harsh enough to grate cheese."

The room erupts with laughter as if grating cheese is the funniest thing anyone has ever heard. Everyone seems to be having fun, but to me it really is too harsh. Shouldn't we be congratulating one another?

Duncan scrapes some ice off his skates and throws it at Charlie. Charlie retaliates by throwing his ball of sock tape at Seven. Next thing you know, the dressing room's bursting with noise, and equipment's flying everywhere. Most of my goalie gear's too heavy to throw, but I toss my knee pads at Fartsby and Dyne.

It turns into a proper celebration, and I'm totally part of it now. I glance over at Hunter. He doesn't look happy. Maybe because for once he's got nothing to throw.

CHAPTER 13

After a brutal practice on Tuesday, Coach Matt takes us to Tim Hortons on the way home. While we scarf down donuts, he tells me about a figure-skating clinic. "Duncan's going. You interested?"

The sweet taste in my mouth turns sour. Coach Matt wouldn't be suggesting something so radical if I'd actually stayed on my feet during practice. "*Figure skating?*"

"Lots of hockey players do it. It's really good for improving your edges."

It has to be good if Duncan is doing it. Still, all I can think of is *Battle of the Blades*, that reality show where professional hockey players get paired with figure skaters to do stuff like double axels and death spirals—just to make them look bad. The last thing I need to do is look worse in skates than I already do.

"What about the Smokies' development clinic?" Duncan says through a mouthful of chocolate glazed. "They have a special thing for goalies."

Getting tips from Junior A players sounds a lot better than a figure-skating clinic. But truthfully, I need both. I know I got lucky with both of my wins.

The way I played in practice today…that's the real me.

But it doesn't matter. There's no way Mom and Dad will sign me up for extra clinics.

"I think it's full, but I can find out." Coach Matt wipes his hands on a napkin. "Do you think your parents will agree?"

"I'll ask," I say, even though I know I won't.

When I get home, there's a note for me on the kitchen table from Mom.

Hi, Elliot,

Hope you had a good day. Have a snack and don't forget to:

1. Do your homework.

2. Call Grandpa.

Love you,

Mom

I decide to call Grandpa first. I can hear Dad sanding wood in his studio, so I grab the laptop from the charging station in the den and take it to my room. When Grandpa appears on the screen, his eyes look tired and his hair's a mess.

Before I can ask him what's wrong, he asks me the same question. "There's worry in your face, Sport," he adds.

I tell him how bad I was at practice. How it makes no sense that I've won not just one game but two.

"Are there any differences between how you prepare for a game and how you prepare for practice?" he asks.

I glance at the bobbleheads lining my dresser. My eyes drift to the table beside my bed, where the Carey Price biography lies on top of a stack of hockey books.

"Well, there is one thing." I hesitate, trying to figure out how to explain. "After we talked, you know, before the game against the Rebels…"

Grandpa cups his ear and aims it toward the screen. "Speak up, Sport! These old ears aren't as sharp as they used to be."

I clear my throat even though I know there's nothing blocking it. I'm talking quietly because I can't believe I'm about to say what I'm about to say. And I don't want anyone but Grandpa to hear it. "I made a wish on the Carey Price bobblehead. I wished for a win. And I think it came true."

Grandpa's ear still fills the screen. I want to see his face. He must think I'm being ridiculous. I know he doesn't look down on people who believe in superstitions and good-luck charms—not like Hunter and the others on my team—but magic?

I rush in to fill the silence. "Not that I believe it's magic or anything. It's just that I talked to the bobblehead before my second game too. So I guess I've got a new superstition."

"Who knows, Sport? Maybe it was the wish and maybe it was you. Either way, you're sure to have good days and bad days. Sure as the setting sun. Don't be so hard on yourself. Stepping into the net for the first time at your age is tough."

My throat feels tight. I'm relieved he didn't laugh at me for thinking what I was thinking. But I don't want to keep talking about it, so I change the subject. "Speaking of skates, I need new ones. My old ones are too small. They make my feet hurt."

"Did you ask your parents?"

As soon as Grandpa says this, I regret saying anything. Dad won't be happy if he finds out I'm telling people about our money trouble.

"Yes. I'll get new ones soon. I'm trying to earn some money so I can help pay for them."

Grandpa's eyes narrow, making the wrinkles around them fold into lines that remind me of the clefts on the chin of Thanos from The Avengers (although I can only ever imagine Grandpa as one of the good guys).

We talk for a bit longer about the difference between regular skates and goalie skates. Grandpa tells me to "put all my eggs in one basket" and get goalie skates. I'm not sure we'll be able to afford them. But his confidence in me means everything.

Grandpa starts yawning, so we say goodbye. It's pretty late in Montreal, but I wish he didn't have to go. Talking to him always makes me feel good. Plus the next thing on Mom's to-do list is homework.

I wander over to my dresser and pick up my Carey Price bobblehead. Turning it over, I try to convince myself that it's really just a hunk of plastic. But if it did grant wishes, I'd ask for Grandpa to live closer. "I wish—"

Out of the corner of my eye, I see Aislyn's shadow pass by my doorway. I drop the bobblehead and cough. I didn't realize my door was open. Did she see me with the bobblehead? Did she hear what I said to Grandpa?

"Hey, Aislyn!"

She turns back when she hears my voice. She doesn't look happy. And she's carrying something that belongs in the kitchen, not her room. Instead of trying to figure out what she might have seen and heard, I point at it. "What's that?" I ask.

"An old toaster," Aislyn replies with a shrug. "Duh."

"I know it's a toaster. I mean, why do you have it?"

"My project for the Change Climate Change contest isn't going well. The bioreactor made more mold than energy."

"So you're making toast instead?"

"Ha ha." Aislyn clearly doesn't think my joke was that clever. "I was trying to generate enough energy to power a small kitchen appliance with the bioreactor. I found this old one in the basement. But I don't need it anymore, so I'm putting it back."

"Can you drop this off in the den on your way?" I hold out the laptop.

Aislyn looks down at it like it's made of toxic waste. "You used it last. You put it away."

I'm still worried that she overheard my confession about the bobblehead. I imagine her laughing about it with her maker-space friends. But getting into an argument with her about the laptop isn't going to help. Hopefully she was too wrapped up in her own problems to notice me talking to a bobblehead about mine.

I toss the laptop on my bed. "So you're giving up on the contest?"

"Of course not! I've got an idea for a solar water heater. I'm going to see if I can find any stuff in the basement."

"You think there's a bunch of junk just hanging around in the basement waiting for you to turn it into something that can save the world? Sounds like a waste of time to me."

Aislyn stares at me hard. "The Change Climate Change contest is not a waste of time."

I didn't mean that the project was a waste of time. But judging by the look on her face, Aislyn's taken it that way.

"You know what is?" she continues. "Hockey!"

Now Aislyn's not the only one upset. I clench my fists. "Hockey's not a waste of time."

"It's not just a waste of time, it's terrible for the environment. Do you have any idea how much energy it takes to maintain an ice rink? Plus it wastes water and pollutes the environment."

"Yeah, well, I don't care! I love hockey. And I already have two wins! Not bad for a rookie goalie."

Aislyn puts her hands on her hips. "Hmmph. Sounds like you got lucky to me. If your team hadn't got so many goals, you'd be"—she glances at the silver box in her hands—"toast."

I didn't think my sister knew anything about my hockey. For some reason, the fact that she does makes me even angrier. And more convinced that she overheard my conversation with Grandpa. "Why don't you just leave me alone!"

"Fine!" Before I can slam the door in her face, Aislyn storms away. But not before adding, "Have fun playing with your dolls!"

CHAPTER 14

I need to start working on my math homework, but it's hard to concentrate. My sister and I don't fight much—mainly because when I'm mean to her (and I really try hard not to be) she always backs off. She didn't today, which must mean she's really worried about the contest.

The bobblehead is still lying on the floor where I dropped it. I pick it up. "Do you have a sister?"

The head nods up and down like it's saying yes, and I'm sure I didn't move it. It's been a while since I read the Carey Price book but I'm pretty sure he does have a sister—just like me. I wonder how his sister feels about having a brother who's so good at what he does.

Placing the bobblehead back on my dresser, I feel my anger melting into sympathy. Aislyn's probably really frustrated that her project isn't going well. Failure is something I know a lot about.

Still, I wish she hadn't mentioned luck. And so what if there was some luck to my wins? I mean, everyone believes in luck—that's why we wish people good luck, or call it bad luck when something goes wrong. Following a superstition is just a way of making sure luck works for you. Some of my teammates might think my rituals are silly, but lots of people have them. Even NASA engineers—firm believers in the scientific method—pass around lucky peanuts when launching a new mission.

I'm wondering whether everyone thinks my wins were just luck when Dad calls us down to dinner. Five fish tacos later, I'm still thinking about it. Mom and Dad spend the whole meal trying to cheer up Aislyn about her project. "You always find a way to rise to the top," Dad says to her.

Later, back in my room, I hear muffled sounds coming through the wall that connects my bedroom to Mom and Dad's. They're arguing about something, but I can't tell what. At one point I'm sure I hear Dad say the word *hockey*. And *waste*. Or maybe it's *taste*. Either way, Grandpa must've said something to Mom about my skates.

I put on my headphones and try to block them out by watching a YouTube channel I've become obsessed with because it has lots of great goalie videos. While I watch, I cross my fingers behind my back. If Mom and Dad are fighting about skates, I'll do anything I can to help win the argument for buying me new ones.

Eventually I give up and put my worksheets—mostly still blank—into my backpack. I tiptoe to the bathroom, feeling like an intruder in my own house. Mom and Dad's bedroom door is closed. Aislyn's bedroom door is closed. Dad likes us to keep them closed to save on heating costs, but I still feel like I've been shut out.

I go back to my room and close the door behind me. A whoosh of air makes my bobbleheads dance. I wonder again if talking to Carey Price is just another silly superstition or whether there's more to it. The only thing I know for sure is that my luck is sure to run out…eventually.

I never find out what Grandpa said to Mom and Dad about skates. Or if he said anything at all. But it doesn't matter. I need new ones, and I can't wait any longer.

I tackle the neighbor's leaf pile after school the next day. Thanks to the first snowfall of the year—just enough to make people serious about cleaning up their yards before it's too late—I pick up some extra jobs raking other lawns as well.

At the end of the week I show Mom how much money I've earned. My finger-crossing must have worked, because she agrees to take me shopping. "If you don't have enough, we'll cover the rest."

"I thought there was no room on the credit card?"

"We paid a bit off at the start of November," she says. "The store had a few big sales last month."

I breathe a bit easier knowing her store's still doing well despite all the hours Mom's spending on her campaign. I know as soon as we get to the sports store that there's no way I'm getting goalie skates, though. They're a lot more expensive than regular skates, and I'm not comfortable asking Mom to pitch in that much.

The pimple-faced salesclerk sees me checking out the price tags and tries to talk me into it. "If you play in net, you need goalie skates. These ones have a clip on the toe so you don't have to tie the pads under the blade."

"We don't know how long Elliot will be in net," Mom says. "And you can't wear goalie skates to play other positions, right, honey?"

I think about Grandpa's advice to put "all my eggs in one basket." But I know she's right.

I pick out a pair of Vapor skates. They fit well—especially after they've been heat molded—and there's even room in the ends to wiggle my toes. They might not be as good as goalie skates, but they're a heck of a lot better than what I'm wearing now.

"Thanks, Mom. I'm sure the new skates are going to help a ton," I say on the way home. "Any chance you can come watch me in action tomorrow?"

"Wish I could, hon," she says. "But things are so—"

"—busy, I know, with the election and stuff…" I let my voice trail off because I don't want her to feel bad. I got new skates. That's enough for now.

When Mom and I get home from the store, I call Duncan. "Want to go to the public skate?"

"I thought you hated public skates."

I did complain about them last winter. But that's just because I went to so many. "I need to work in my new skates before the game tomorrow. The blades are still pretty sharp even though we asked the salesclerk not to sharpen them."

"Glad you got new skates. But I can't go to the public skate tonight. Sorry, Elliot."

"What?" Duncan and I almost always hang out on Friday nights. "Why?"

"Hunter's here."

Something flares in my chest like a match has just been lit. "What's Hunter doing there?"

"His dad wanted to talk to my dad. No biggie."

For a second I think about asking if Hunter wants to come with us. But he'd probably just make fun of me. For the way I line up all my gear in order before putting it on. Or for the way I skate when I finally get on the ice. Or both. "Okay. See you tomorrow, I guess."

"See you tomorrow."

After hanging up, I wander around my room, wondering whether Duncan and Hunter are playing mini sticks in his basement. Or playing video games if Hunter's knee is still bad. Which it must be since he's not back on the ice yet.

When *will* he be back on the ice? Will my luck run out before then? Or do I still have time to prove that I belong?

I walk over to my dresser and pick up the Carey Price bobblehead. "How about helping me out again?"

The head bobbles back.

"Tomorrow I'd like a shutout."

CHAPTER 15

Early the next morning we face the Grand Forks Bruins—the only undefeated team in the league besides us. Jerry-Horn's calling it our first real battle of the season. Most of the Blazers are totally pumped.

Not me. Although my skates feel pretty good, I'd rather give them their first ride in net against a team that's not quite so strong.

It's going to take a miracle to get me through my third game between the pipes. As I go through warm-up I remember the words I whispered to my bobblehead. I can't believe I thought it was possible. Even with all the magic in the world, a shutout for me is as unlikely as the Maple Leafs winning another Stanley Cup.

From the first face-off, the Bruins play rough. And their rough play doesn't stop after the whistle. They poke us with their sticks and chirp at us like birds—scavenger birds with dirty mouths.

I heard some of the chatter last season. But it was never directed at me (even the meanest hockey players leave the pathetic ones alone). Now that it is, I really feel like part of the action.

Actually I couldn't be more part of the action. Pucks come at me from every direction. Some hit me, some don't. The ones that do bounce off without doing much damage.

The other Blazers are slow to respond to the intensity of the Bruins. There are lots of turnovers in the neutral zone and scrimmages along the boards, but we don't take many shots. The first period ends 0–0.

"You're playing great, Elliot," Coach Tibor says to me during the break. "There must've been something special in your cornflakes this morning."

I grin, wondering what Carey Price eats for breakfast.

"They're getting away with murder out there," Coach Lisa says as we hover around the bench. "Murder! The officials aren't calling anything!"

"These refs have no idea what they're doing!" Hunter says this so loud it's like he's hoping they'll overhear him. I'm pretty sure this isn't the kind of help we need from Hunter on the bench.

Coach Tibor puts a hand on his shoulder. "There's no point making them mad. Then we'll never get any breaks."

I'm glad Coach Tibor spoke up but also annoyed. He's supposed to be worrying about me, not Hunter the injured goaltender. I guess I should just be happy Hunter's still on the bench and I'm still in net. For now, anyway.

"We're not going to let the referees dictate our game," says Coach Matt. "And just because the other team is playing rough, that doesn't mean we have to become brutes. Stick with the game plan."

This lasts for a while. But by the end of the second, my teammates are getting frustrated. There's no room to move on the ice because the Bruins aren't afraid to use their bodies to knock us down and steal the puck.

Me? I'm feeling great, making saves I never thought I could make. It's like I belong in net. I know it sounds silly— even to me—but it's like I've got Carey Price standing guard on both of my posts.

Still, I can't help wishing someone in my family was here to see it.

Early in the third, Jerry-Horn gets elbowed in the corner. He picks up his stick with both hands and cross-checks the Bruins player in the chest. The ref, who's not much older than me, finally calls a penalty.

"Oh sure, now you figure out how to use your whistle!" Coach Lisa shouts.

A Bruins coach yells back, and pretty soon the parents are getting into it too.

I try to block them out and concentrate on the penalty kill. I've gotten through two whole periods without allowing a goal. But now we're down a player—I'm going to need a miracle to keep the puck out of the net.

Tapping the goalposts with my stick—not so hard that I get knocked over—I shout, "Come on, Blazers!"

Madder loses the draw. Almost instantly the Bruins left winger comes crashing toward me. Their center parks himself in the crease. I try to look around him but can't get a good view of the play. Duncan comes in and tries to push him out.

The guy's a tank. He doesn't move an inch.

Now there are at least four Bruins in front of me. I can't see anything, but I feel the puck hit my blocker. I glance behind me. There's nothing in the net besides half my body.

The puck must've dropped into the crease after I made the save. I don't know where it is, so I can't fall on top of it. Desperate, I zip my legs together and try to stay on my feet.

There's a bunch of commotion and then suddenly Madder comes up with the puck.

"Ice it!" Duncan and Kali shout at the same time.

Madder has other ideas. With a clear lane he flies up the ice, shorthanded. "Go, Madder," I wheeze, out of breath from all the commotion around my net just a few moments ago.

"All the way!" screams Coach Lisa. "ALL THE WAY!!"

"Hold up!" Coach Matt yells. "Kill time."

Madder slows down, stickhandling while he waits for Dyne to catch up. He makes a pass off the boards. Too late. Dyne's not the only player on the ice who's caught up to Madder.

A Bruins defenseman steals the puck. I steady myself with my stick and try to slow my breathing.

Duncan and Kali skate backward, staying between me and the puck. "Close the gap," yells Coach Tibor.

They do. But the Bruins forwards are fast, and before I know it, one of them has snuck past the defense. The puck carrier passes it ahead to his teammate, who unleashes a one-timer. It's a bottle rocket. In the net before I can even blink.

My heart dive-bombs into my new skates. So much for the shutout.

I dig the puck out and then turn to get my water bottle from the top of the net. There's a commotion at the blue line. The linesman blows his whistle and waves his arms. "Offside!"

"NO GOAL!" The referee slices his hands through the air like he's chopping off heads.

"What?" The face of the Bruins coach is so white it looks like his head really has been chopped off. He starts yelling a bunch of words we're not supposed to say, including a few I've never heard before. The referee looks scared, but the linesman (who's probably twice as old as the ref) skates over and calmly makes his point. Since there's no video replay or anything, the linesman's call stands.

No goal.

CHAPTER 16

The game totally changes after that. Kali breaks the 0–0 tie with a soft goal from a sharp angle. My teammates turn up the heat and stay hot for the rest of the period. When the horn blows to end the game, it's 7–0.

The Blazers on the ice drop their sticks and skate straight toward me. The Blazers on the bench join them. I get buried under a pile of players so thick I can barely breathe.

And I don't care. My wish came true!

When I finally get up, my legs are so wobbly I can barely skate to the bench. I glance up at the scoreboard and take a picture of it in my mind.

"Everyone contributed to that win. Great work, Blazers!" Coach Matt goes around patting us each on the back even though we're all covered in sweat. He has praise for everyone.

"Great offense. Even better defense. Good job in net, Elliot. And way to support your team, Hunter."

Kali leaves to change when the coaches do. Jerry-Horn pumps the music until I can't tell whether it's my heart or the music that's beating so loud. "This should be our win song," he announces.

Everyone voices their agreement by singing along to the chorus. We sound like a bunch of dying frogs—happy dying frogs.

It's happiness I've never felt before. If I wasn't waiting for Hunter to say something negative about me and my play, this moment would be perfect.

"Looks like you could be out of a job, Hunter," someone says during the break between songs.

I flinch, expecting a quick and nasty comeback from Hunter. But he doesn't respond.

"If you don't come back soon, maybe we won't need you anymore," Gray adds.

"Ouch," says Seven.

"Maybe you can be our mascot." Fartsby makes this suggestion with a totally straight face.

"What does a Blazer look like?"

"Portland's mascot is called Blaze the Trail Cat," says Charlie. "But it looks more like a squirrel on steroids."

Madder laughs. "Good one, Charlie!"

"The Flyers have the creepiest mascot," says Fartsby.

"Gritty!" Seven exclaims. "What's that big hairy orange creature supposed to be, anyway?"

"Dunno," says Gray. "But the one that freaks me out is Stinger for the Columbus Blue Jackets."

Jerry-Horn smiles. "That's just 'cause you're scared of bees, Gray-Man."

"Who isn't?" Gray replies with a grin.

The dressing room erupts as my teammates offer up the names of bizarre mascots. Then they move on to weird team names. Charlie gives examples from minor-league base-ball—Trash Pandas, Yard Goats and Sod Poodles.

I stay silent, mostly because everyone knows this stuff so much better than I do. But also because I'm still worrying about what will happen when Hunter comes back.

Judging from the serious look on Hunter's face, I bet that's what he's thinking about too.

"You should've seen it, Mom. The celebration after the game was epic."

Mom pulls the van over to the side of the road. "Epic?"

I jump out and grab an *Esme Feldner-Martel for Mayor* sign from the back. After I'm done staking it into the ground, I hop back into the van. "Yep, it was wild. The music was loud and everyone was having fun, trash-talking and stuff—"

Mom's eyebrows shoot up. She hates trash talk.

"Well, not really trash-talking, but teasing, you know?"

To be honest, I don't always know the difference between trash-talking, teasing and bullying. It's nice not being the butt of the joke all the time. But I still think my teammates often take it too far—not just with me, with everyone.

We get to the next stop. Mom puts on the hazard lights. I jump out and hammer in another sign. It's a warm day for November, and I'm starting to work up a sweat. The dusting of snow that fell earlier has melted, and most of the grass is still green.

"Then Charlie got a nosebleed. You should've seen it, Mom. There was blood everywhere. When we tried to help him, we all got into a water fight and—"

"I hope you cleaned it up."

"Of course we did." Which is true, if you count throwing paper towels around as cleaning up.

Mom pulls over again and we repeat the routine. We've been at this for a while now, and it's starting to feel as automatic as the drills we do in practice. I hadn't expected helping Mom to be so fun. It doesn't matter that I haven't gotten any new raking or shoveling jobs—seeing Mom's excitement is good enough. The election's getting closer, and she seems determined to win.

"Then we went to Boston Pizza," I continue. "We had two huge tables. One for the parents and one for the kids."

"I'm sorry I wasn't there," Mom says after I've finished telling her every detail, right down to Dyne and Gray polishing off an entire extra-large pizza. Each. "Remind me to pay Coach Matt back."

"Will do." I salute before jumping out of the van.

Another stop, another sign. This time, just as I'm about to get back into the van, a voice calls out, "Hey, kid! What do you think you're doing?" The guy strides toward me. The door on the apartment building behind him is still swinging. "You can't put that junk on my property!"

I look down. A sidewalk separates the grass I'm standing on from the scruffy lawn in front of the building.

"I think this part's public?" I begin.

Mom steps out of the van. "Sorry, sir. We didn't mean to upset you."

"I would never vote for you anyway." He shakes his head. "Beekeeping within city limits? That's the last thing we need!"

"I hear what you're saying. If you have a few minutes, I'd be happy to go over the details of my proposal—"

"I DO NOT have a few minutes."

"I understand." Mom stands tall, her spine as straight as a hockey stick. "Elliot, can you please remove the sign from this gentleman's yard?"

Hands shaking, I grab the bottom of the stake and pull it out. The ground smells like dog poo.

I gag.

Without another word, Mom ushers me into the van and pulls away. We drive for a while not talking, until Mom finally says, "I'm sorry you experienced that, honey."

"*You're* sorry?" All the emotion I've bottled up comes pouring out. "It's that *jerk* who should be sorry! We weren't doing anything wrong!"

"He's entitled to his opinion." Mom sighs. "That's how democracy works."

"Maybe. But he didn't have to be so rude about it." Chewing my fingernail, I stare out the van window at the smelter, which employs half of Trail, and the large smokestacks the Trail Smoke Eaters are named after. The sun's beginning to set behind a thin layer of cloud. A day that started so bright has gone dark.

"How could you just stand there while he yelled at you?" I ask. "You were so calm."

"Politics is a long game, Elliot. Making change requires a lot of time and patience. It takes perseverance and resilience."

Resilience is one of Mom's favorite words. She says it is the key to success in life. But I don't think I have as much of it as I should. "I could never do that," I say.

"Yes, you could."

I cross my arms over my chest, ready for another speech about managing my emotions and controlling my temper. Instead she surprises me by adding, "And you do."

"What?"

"Think about what you've accomplished in hockey. Staying in the game last season even though you struggled. And then this year stepping up to be goalie. That takes a lot of courage."

Courage. I never thought of it that way. I like the sound of it. But I don't know what it has to do with a mean guy who hates bees. "I guess."

Mom gives me a tired smile. Then she turns back to the road. I keep expecting her to make another stop—there are still signs in the back of the van—but she doesn't.

We just go straight home.

CHAPTER 17

With all the excitement of the weekend, I totally forget to do my math homework. Again. I try to get it done over lunch, but we're all having so much fun talking hockey that it slips my mind.

During math class Mr. Morrisette walks around collecting our assignments. I look up at him and shake my head. "Busy with hockey. Sorry."

Mr. Morrisette frowns. But he's a hockey player—he coaches his daughter's team and used to play goal for the Smokies— so I'm sure he understands.

In English, the last class of the day, an announcement comes over the PA. "Would Elliot Feldner-Martel please come to the office?"

I'm in the middle of doing a free write on our shutout against the Bruins. I continue scribbling away, ignoring the curious glances of my classmates.

Since English is almost over, I assume that whatever's waiting for me at the office can wait till the bell. I'm not the kind of kid who gets in trouble, so it's probably a message from Mom. Or maybe the hoodie I just realized I left behind in gym class got turned in to the office.

But when Ms. Deadmarsh comes over to excuse me before she's assigned reading chapters for homework, my stomach flips. This is bigger than a note from Mom. Or a lost sweater.

My fears are confirmed when I walk into the office. The secretary—not smiling like she usually does—points to the principal's door. "They're waiting for you in there."

They?

Our principal, Ms. Kuhn, sits behind her desk. The room smells of pencil shavings and Play-Doh.

Facing her is Mr. Morrisette, and sitting next to him is my dad. As I enter the room, I don't look either of them in the eye. I can't.

"Have a seat, Elliot," says Ms. Kuhn. "I assume you know what this meeting's about?"

I perch on the edge of the only empty chair in the room, putting my hands under my knees so I won't bite my nails. "School?"

Ms. Kuhn rests her chin on her hand. "What about school?"

Staring at the glass bowl of candy on her desk, I wonder how many times my gifted sister has sat in this office, meeting with teachers and learning specialists to talk about all the good stuff she's done (or is going to do). It doesn't take a genius to figure out what Ms. Kuhn's thinking now: *How can Elliot be so dumb when his sister's so smart?*

"Come on, E," Dad finally snaps. "Don't waste everyone's time. We're here because you're not doing your schoolwork."

Things move quickly from there. After showing Dad the results of my last two tests, Mr. Morrisette hands him a stack of incomplete homework. *Traitor.*

Ms. Deadmarsh isn't here because she's on bus duty, but Ms. Kuhn cheerfully fills Dad in on the English assignments I've missed too. As bad as I'm doing in English and math, my other subjects are going okay—science (because we do labs in class), social studies (because Mr. Flemming doesn't give homework) and gym (for obvious reasons). That's more than half my subjects—see, I can do math—but you'd think I was failing everything by the depth of Dad's scowl.

By the time the meeting's over, the hallways are empty and the buses are gone. I get my backpack from my locker and wait for Dad to pick me up at the front of the school. I'm pacing the empty sidewalk, wondering why he had to park so far away, when Hunter appears out of nowhere. He's not using crutches anymore, but he still walks with a limp.

"What's up, Jelly? You get lucky when it comes to stopping the puck but can't save yourself from detention?"

"I wasn't in detention," I mumble. "Were you?"

Hunter drags the toe of his injured leg across the sewer grate. "No. My dad would kill me if I got detention."

This might not be an exaggeration. I've heard the way Hunter's dad talks to him in public. Once, when I was watching Duncan's game a couple years ago, I even saw Hunter's dad grab Hunter by the jersey and pull him off the ice for a "quiet" talk between periods. I can't imagine what happens when they're behind closed doors.

I've always wished for a dad who cares about hockey. But I'd never trade my dad for a dad as mean as Hunter's.

"Why are you here so late then?" I ask.

I'm surprised when Hunter starts telling me about the extra tutoring he gets—not because his grades are bad but because his dad is already thinking about university hockey scholarships. Hunter's interrupted when his dad pulls up in their fancy SUV. He honks the horn repeatedly. As Hunter steps toward the vehicle, his dad rolls down the window.

"Stop limping," he barks. "You'll mess up your recovery, you fool!"

Before Hunter's even done up his seat belt, his dad peels away from the curb, showering me in a cloud of exhaust. When my dad finally appears, I'm still trembling over how harshly Hunter's dad spoke to him. I crawl into the van. The back is full of Dad's wood samples. I realize that I didn't just drag him away from the studio. I dragged him away from appointments and potential sales he's had set up for weeks. He could have yelled at me. But he doesn't.

"I'm sorry, Dad."

Dad grips the steering wheel. "I'm very disappointed, E. School is important. It's your job right now. If hockey is taking up so much time that you can't get your homework done, then maybe you shouldn't be playing."

I did use hockey as an excuse with Mr. Morrisette. And it's true that I've been more distracted this year. But if Dad blames hockey, he'll make me quit for sure.

"It has nothing to do with hockey."

"Then I don't get it." Dad shakes his head. "You're smart, E, and I expect more from you. I don't want you to make the same mistakes I did when I was younger."

"What mistakes?"

"I didn't take school seriously because I wanted to become an artist." Dad glances at me like he's measuring my reaction. It's the same way I looked at Grandpa after I told him I believed in bobblehead magic. "Now I wish I'd paid more attention in math and…all those other subjects I considered a waste of time."

"Then you wouldn't be doing what you're doing." I take a deep breath. The air smells the same as in our house—like fresh-cut wood. A smell I find comforting. "And you're a good artist. Everyone wishes they could afford one of your carvings."

"Maybe. It's hard to support a family as an artist, though. Even if you're a good one." Somewhere behind us a car honks, startling us both. Dad smiles at me before pulling forward. "But thanks for saying that, E."

Dad and I don't talk like this. It makes me feel exposed, like a hockey player without a helmet. But it also makes me feel close to him.

"I mean it, Dad. I'm glad you didn't give up on your dreams."

"And I don't want you to give up on yours." Dad clears his throat, and for a moment I think I see tears in his eyes. "I just don't want you to limit your options. And not doing well in school can do that."

My throat feels tight as I focus on the road ahead. "I'll try, Dad. I promise."

CHAPTER 18

I do try to do better at school. It's just that hockey practice and public skate and dryland training (following a new
routine Duncan sent me), not to mention watching goalie
videos and reading hockey books, take up a lot of my time.
We have our first tournament on the weekend, and I want—
no, I *need*—to be ready.

One night I'm looking up information for an English essay
on the guy who invented Velcro (a topic I chose because hockey
equipment was revolutionized by Velcro) when I'm hit with an
idea that Ms. Deadmarsh would call *out-of-the-box thinking*.

I race down to the basement and grab the old toaster from
a shelf of random things that aren't quite broken enough to
throw away. I'm back in my room fiddling around with it—
trying to figure out if I can get it to shoot pucks instead of
bread—when I hear shouting downstairs.

"Every parent had to sign up for a volunteer slot!" Mom
yells. "And I have a fundraising event."

"You're the one who went along with Elliot playing hockey.
Between the house, the kids and the store, I'm covering enough
of your commitments. I have my own job, you know!"

"It's only a two-hour slot, for goodness' sake!"

Even though they're yelling at each other, I feel like I'm the one being attacked. I count the dirty clothes on my floor—*1, shirt, 2, jeans, 3, sweater, 4, underwear, 5, sock, 6, sock, 7 sock…*

I pick up one of the socks and throw it against my door. It doesn't make me feel any better than the counting.

Their fights always upset me, but this one's worse. Mom's dealing with enough angry people in her run for mayor. And it's not just the bee-hater. Aislyn told me she's also been getting some nasty emails. I don't want to add to Mom's stress.

Plus since Dad met with my teachers and we had that talk in the car, I've been noticing just how hard he works. I don't want to add to that either.

But I think what makes me feel so lousy is that I'm excited about the tournament. The only thing better than playing a game is playing multiple games in a row, with time to hang out with my team in between. It sucks that my family is so *not* excited about it.

Instead of crossing and uncrossing my fingers, I go over to my bobblehead collection and pick up Carey Price. We stare at each other as the voices of my parents die down.

"I bet your parents are super proud of you," I whisper.

Mom's voice breaks the silence. "Fine! I'll do the shift!"

"Bloody right!" Dad yells back.

I feel bad that Mom will have to miss her fundraising event. But I'm glad she'll be at the arena for the tournament. Because I really, really want her to see me play.

More than anything, I want to make her proud. But I can't shake this sinking feeling that my luck has already run out.

"Hey, Pricer." I speak slowly as I try to figure out how I can make not just Mom but *both* of my parents proud. How do I show them that hockey is not a waste of time—mine or theirs?

Finally it comes to me. "How 'bout another shutout this weekend?"

Running my finger over the plastic jersey, I have another thought. If Mom only has to do a two-hour shift, there's no telling what game she might see. And who knows when—or if—Dad will ever make it to the arena.

"Actually—how about a shutout in every game?"

We get to leave school early on Friday for our first game of the tournament, against the Spokane Eagles. Since Trail's hosting the event, we don't have to travel or stay in a hotel (both things I loved doing last season for our two out-of-town tournaments), but at least we get the afternoon draw. Playing hockey is even more exciting when everyone else is still at school learning about ancient civilizations.

Judging from the noise in our dressing room, I'm not the only one who feels this way. The electricity's so strong we practically melt the ice during warm-up.

As I set out my gear in the right order, I think about the wish I made on the bobblehead. I found out over breakfast that Mom's not going to be at this game. But that didn't stop me from reminding Carey Price about the shutouts.

Thanks to Grandpa, I now ask the bobblehead for luck every time I'm going on the ice. It doesn't matter if it's a game or a practice. Since Coach Matt picked us up from school, I'm a bit worried about the amount of time that's passed. It seems like ages since I left my bedroom this morning.

During the pre-game talk Coach Matt warns us that the Eagles are strong this year. We find out as soon as we take the ice that he's not wrong. But from the first face-off, the Blazers are on fire.

Our forwards attack the zone relentlessly in the first and second periods. The only thing that keeps the Eagles in the game is their goalie. He makes some impossible saves, including one where he's pretty much standing on his head—for real.

At the other end of the ice, our defense shines. They don't let the Eagles get in deep very often. When they do, someone's always there to clear away the rebound.

We back off in the third as the coaches put my teammates in different positions—forwards try playing defense, wingers try playing center, and defense tries forward. I'm extra glad to be in goal because I don't have to switch. Mastering one position's tough enough for me.

Even though I want my teammates to do well, it's kind of nice to see other Blazers struggling to learn a new place on the ice. The only one who's good at every position is Kali. On defense—her usual spot—she controls the point better than ever and gets an assist on almost every goal. On offense she knows when to hold back and when to let loose. She gets two goals and three assists for the game.

We beat them 5–0.

After the game we line up to hear Coach Matt give out the Player of the Game award to one of the Eagles. No one's surprised when he gives it to their goalie. The score might not show it, but he definitely kept them in the game.

As the Eagles coach takes the mic, it crosses my mind that I could win too. The Eagles goalie won after letting in five goals, after all, and I got a shutout. No one else in the arena knows that I might've had help from a bobblehead.

"First I want to thank Trail for hosting this tournament," says the Eagles coach. "This was not the way we wanted to start off, but the bounces were just not going our way today."

I never won Player of the Game last season. Not once. I did win the golden jersey, a thing they do in U11 to acknowledge the hardest-working player on the ice after every game. But everyone eventually wins the golden jersey. It's how coaches keep kids motivated.

"This player pulled out all the stops. I've never seen someone cover so much ground in one game. The entire Trail team played well, but this person shut us down from every angle."

Come on! Coach Matt didn't give a speech before he named the Eagles Player of the Game. The longer this drags out, the more I think it just might be possible for me to win.

"The Player of the Game for the Trail Blazers is…"

The pounding in my head is so loud, I have to strain to hear.

"Katherine Solnyskina!"

CHAPTER 19

I feel stupid for thinking I had a chance to win. I don't have long to dwell on it, though, because Coach Matt sends us home quickly with instructions to get to bed by nine—which, based on the groans in the dressing room, is next to impossible for some of my teammates.

Not for me, though. I'm beyond exhausted and want to get a good night's sleep before our game against the Revelstoke Grizzlies super early the next morning.

I'm awake before my alarm goes off but still have to rush to get ready. I try to keep quiet because everyone else is still in bed.

When my bag is packed and waiting outside the front door, I quickly run to my bedroom before Coach Matt arrives to pick me up. I grab the bobblehead. "Same as always, Pricer. Only this time I need double luck since I won't make it home between games. And the shutout wish is super important today because Mom's shift at the arena is this afternoon. Thanks for your help!"

In the dressing room everyone's quiet—even Jerry-Horn. I appreciate the silence because it helps me focus on my routine. Even though I don't have to go, I hit the bathroom first. Since the game against the Leafs—when I didn't play well because I had to pee—I always go before getting dressed. I'm not hungry either, but I make sure to eat one granola bar from the box I keep in my bag before putting on the piece of equipment that always goes last—my mask.

The game starts slowly, as if the sluggishness from the dressing room has followed us onto the ice. No matter how loud Coach Lisa yells, no one seems to wake up. No one except Seven, who scores two goals in the first period. There are no goals in the second, but Seven adds two more in the third. I don't think there's a term for getting four goals in one game, but there should be. Not that any slang could ever explain just how well Seven played. Especially since his last goal came from the perfect deflection of a saucer shot made by Gray. I bet some NHL players couldn't direct a puck as good as Seven did on that play.

Final score, 4–0.

The officials rush us into position for the awards ceremony because the Zamboni's waiting to clear the ice. This works for me because I'm anxious to get off the ice as well. It's not like I'm going to win Player of the Game, and besides, I like hanging out with my teammates between games. There's always fun stuff to do, like passing the puck around outside the dressing room, loading up on carbs and watching other teams play.

While Coach Lisa's giving out Player of the Game for the Grizzlies, I glance up at the bleachers to make sure Seven's family is here to see him win. I don't see them, but I do see Mom.

She's standing at the boards, clutching her reusable coffee mug. I'm so startled to see her, I almost fall over.

She gives me a small wave. I smile back.

How long has she been watching? Did I make any good saves while she was here? I really hope she saw the last one, where I robbed the Grizzlies center when he tried to tuck one through the five-hole.

Coach Lisa hands the mic to the Grizzlies coach. Unlike the Eagles coach, he wastes no time.

"Player of the Game for the Blazers," he says, "is Rashid Abdullah!"

It's not hard to spot Seven's family in the stands now. They are the ones hopping up and down and waving their arms furiously. I'm happy for him, but hearing their whistles makes me want to give Mom something to cheer about—even more than I did before.

Mom's waiting for me outside the dressing room. She makes a big deal out of how well I played but doesn't mention the shutout or my great save. Instead she says, "I have to volunteer at the prize table, and I need you to help."

I want to hang out with my teammates. But it's not like I have a choice. Mom's volunteering so I can play hockey. I can't exactly leave her on her own.

We head to the arena lobby and take a seat behind a folded table loaded with an assortment of prize baskets, all overflowing with things nobody really needs. Mom's donated a basket full of stuff from the store (probably things that aren't selling very well).

The lobby's a lot warmer than the rink. When Mom takes off her puffy jacket, I see she's wearing a bright badge that stands out like a beacon in the dimly lit foyer of the arena.

Running for Mayor. Ask if you want to KNOW MORE.

I really hope it doesn't attract too much attention. The last thing either of us needs is another run-in like the one we had with the bee-hater.

There's tons of traffic at the table, especially between games. We sell lots of tournament programs, entries for the toonie stick draw and lottery lollipops. But when the deep fryer gets fired up for lunch, the foyer becomes a ghost town.

My stomach growls as the smell of fat drifts toward us from the concession area. "Can I grab something to eat?"

Mom pulls a bright green twenty from her wallet. "Sure, honey. Can you get a burger and fries for me too, please?"

It's amazing how good fries cooked in dirty grease and charred burgers without much beef in them taste when you're at the arena. I really do love everything about hockey. Even hanging out at the prize table with Mom.

"Oh—you're the woman who's running for mayor."

The woman talking to Mom has her back to me. She's wearing a Trail jersey with *Hockey Mom* embroidered on the back where the player's last name usually goes.

Why does this have to happen just when things were going well? I bite my fingernail and taste the ketchup I was enjoying so much just a minute ago.

"Esme Feldner-Martel." Mom smiles. "Nice to meet you."

Even though Mom doesn't extend her hand—no one really does that anymore—the woman steps back as if Mom might be contagious. "Our sons are on the same team. I'm Nico's mom, Tina Escobar."

I move closer to Mom's end of the table. I recognize the woman from the group of Blazers parents who always sit together at games. Nico's the only fifth grader on the team, and it's taken me a while to get to know him. He's super quiet, which is why everyone calls him Mouse. His mom, however, is louder than any other parent in the stands (besides Fartsby's mom, who rings her cowbell like it's an Olympic sport).

"My older son also knows your daughter," Mrs. Escobar continues. "They were in the same physics club this summer. Some type of enrichment for her or something?" Mrs. Escobar makes it sound like a question. To me, it seems more like an accusation.

"Yes, Aislyn was put in the high school group even though she's just started sixth grade." There's just a hint of pride in Mom's voice but to me it sounds like she's speaking through a blowhorn. She didn't sound anywhere near that proud when she congratulated me on my good game this morning.

"I looked at your website. Your daughter's adopted?" Even though I know there's lots of information about my family out there—and it's not like we've got anything to hide—I still wish Mrs. Escobar would stop being so nosy. This is supposed to be my time with Mom.

I stare at the prize table and try to tune them out. But then I hear Mrs. Escobar say, "So Elliot must've been a mistake."

Mistake? Did she just refer to me as a mistake?

Mom shakes her head. "I don't know what you mean."

"Isn't that what always happens? A couple can't conceive so they decide to adopt and next thing you know—" Mrs. Escobar snaps her fingers "—pregnant."

"We adopted Aislyn three years ago." Mom emphasizes "three" just enough to let me know that she's annoyed. But not as annoyed as I am. "And my pregnancy with Elliot was very much planned."

Mrs. Escobar looks at me for the first time. "Well, as much as we can plan these things, I guess!"

I wrap the edge of my shirt around my finger as if I'm trying to stop it from bleeding.

"I guess," Mom says. Her voice is flat.

"Hmm." Mrs. Escobar opens her purse and takes out a bottle of hand sanitizer. "It's a bit unusual that you all have the same hyphenated last name, isn't it? Especially with the wife's name going last?"

That's when I realize that Mrs. Escobar hadn't just read Mom's website—she had studied it.

Mom pinches the bridge of her nose. "Well, Feldner-Martel sounded better than Martel-Feldner, and my husband didn't mind."

Mrs. Escobar drowns her hands in sanitizer as she considers Mom's answer. "Hmm. You must've married quite the feminist."

I never thought of Dad this way. I guess it's true—and I kind of like it.

It looks as if Mrs. Esobar's about to say more when Mom asks, "Would you like to buy a tournament schedule? It comes with twenty tickets. You can use them to enter the draw for any of our wonderful gift baskets."

I drop the edge of my shirt in relief. Mom's good at this politician stuff. I love the way she flipped back to hockey talk.

Still, when Mrs. Escobar finally starts walking away from the prize table—swinging her oversize purse like a weapon—I can't help wishing that Mom had told her to mind her own business.

Especially when Mrs. Escobar turns back and adds, "Hope the next game goes well for you, Elliot. I have a feeling your luck will run out eventually. How can it not? Seems too good to be true."

CHAPTER 20

She's not wrong. My luck *is* too good to be true.

Mom had an answer for all Mrs. Escobar's other questions. Even the one about me being a mistake. But I've got no response to her last one.

How can my luck not run out?

I'm sure others are wondering too. Luckily, most people don't go around saying whatever is on their minds.

What if my teammates are thinking the same thing and just haven't asked? Not about my family—my friends never seem to care about my family's background the way adults do—but about my luck? Are they wondering how their rookie goalie's getting all these shutouts?

What if they find out I'm being fueled by the magic of a bobblehead? Will they think I'm silly for believing in something so far-fetched? Or worse—*desperate* enough to believe in anything at all?

Am I that desperate? Do I actually believe my wishes are coming true?

Being good in goal—and getting shutouts—is supposed to help me fit in. What if it makes me an outcast? Again?

All these thoughts run through my head like a scab I can't stop picking at.

They stay with me through the rest of our shift at the prize table...

And while Duncan and I watch the end of the game before ours...

And while we're in the dressing room getting ready to take on the Osoyoos Coyotes in our last game of the round-robin.

A game we win. With another shutout. Final score, 4–0 Blazers.

I don't sleep well that night. I have a weird dream where my math binder comes to life and starts shouting equations at me. While I'm trying to keep my binder quiet (so no one finds out about some big secret I'm hiding), my Carey Price bobblehead comes to life too. Together they try to attack me—Carey Price with his hockey stick, the binder with pucks that shoot out of its mouth. I can't fight them off and I can't run away. I try screaming for help, but for some reason I can't make a sound.

I wake up in a panic. I squint at Carey Price—standing completely still in the sunlight peeking through my blinds— then at the alarm clock that didn't wake me up. It takes me a minute to remember why I didn't set it.

Winning all three games in the round-robin comes with two big bonuses:

1. We automatically advance to the finals.
2. We don't play till noon.

I could sleep longer, but I'm too rattled. Lured by the smell of bacon, I head down to the kitchen. Dad and Aislyn are at the table, eating breakfast. No sign of Mom. Aislyn tells me she's gone to some election event.

"Can I make you some eggs?" asks Dad.

He's eating what looks like an egg-white omelet full of green stuff. Yuck. Aislyn's got a plateful of scrambled eggs covered in cheese. Double yuck. I'm starving. But Dad never cooks eggs three different ways. "No, thanks."

"You need protein to fuel you through the finals. I'll make them sunny-side up."

I'm a bit surprised he's willing to cook my eggs the way I like them, given how busy he's been. But I'm absolutely shocked he's had time to follow the tournament. It's so great that he knows I'm in the finals. What if there's a chance he can make it to the game?

I decide to risk it. "Are you going to come watch me play?"

"Sorry, E," Dad says as he heats up the frying pan. "I promised Aislyn I'd take her to the shop to get materials for her wind turbine."

The warmth I was feeling evaporates. He might be paying attention, but he'd still rather help Aislyn than watch me play. "What happened to the solar thing?"

"Weren't you listening at dinner last night?" Aislyn rolls her eyes. "The water heater didn't work. So I'm going to see if I can make a wearable wind turbine instead."

Aislyn goes on and on about it as I gobble down the eggs Dad made me. For once I don't mind her stealing the spotlight.

I'm not sure why. Maybe because I don't really want Dad to see how disappointed I am.

When I'm done eating, I go up to my bedroom to get ready. I don't like to think I'm becoming even more superstitious, but I now have a pre-game routine at home too. It starts with a few stretches and ends with a chat between Carey and me.

"Here we go again," I say to the bobblehead. "This is the finals, so I definitely need some luck. We can probably back off on the shutouts, though. No one in my family is going to be there, and me getting so many goose eggs is starting to look supersti—I mean, suspicious."

The doorbell rings before the bobblehead can respond. Not that I expect it to. Duh.

Coach Matt said he'd be back to pick me up early, but I didn't think he'd be here so soon. I don't like to keep him waiting, so I head to the door, sliding down the carpeted stairs as fast as I can.

Game on.

Coach Matt gets Duncan and me to the rink in time to see some of the game between the Fernie Ghostriders (the second-place team in pool A) and the Trail Rebels (the second-place team in pool B). The playoff structure is simple. Whoever wins this game gets the bronze medal, and whoever wins our game gets the gold.

Watching them play, I start to get nervous. Both teams are taking lots of shots and both goalies are kicking them aside like it's nothing. There's no way I can play like that. Especially now that I've changed my wish.

As my teammates trickle into the arena, we head to the dressing room. I've gotten pretty good at putting on the goalie equipment. But my fingers are so sore from biting my nails that I can't strap on my leg pads.

"You okay?" Duncan asks.

I want to ask him if he thinks it's strange that I'm getting all these shutouts. Whether anyone else on the team has mentioned my unbelievable luck. A small part of me even wants to tell him about my bobblehead wishes.

I don't get a chance to do either. Before I can say anything, Kali bursts into the dressing room. "I've got insider information!"

Jerry-Horn turns down the music. "Spill it, Kali. What do you know?"

I force the straps through the buckle of my leg pad. As curious as I am to know what Kali's talking about, I can't stop to listen. Everyone's ready to hit the ice but me.

Kali drops down onto the bench between Seven and Mouse. "Do you guys know Jaswinder Sandhu?"

"Sure, I know Jas," says Charlie. "Goalie for the Wildcats, right?"

The word *goalie* catches my attention for a second. Then I start thinking about the Wildcats—the only all-girls team in our league—and wondering why Kali doesn't play for them instead of us. She's one of our best players, and I'd hate to lose her, but if I were Kali, I'd definitely want to get away from this bunch of smelly, trash-talking boys.

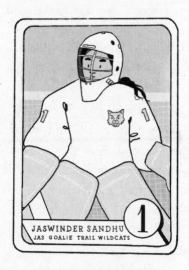

JASWINDER SANDHU
JAS GOALIE TRAIL WILDCATS

Fartsby must have read my mind. "Hey, Kali, why don't you play for the Wildcats?" he asks.

Kali gives Charlie a look that tells me she really wishes she could. "Mom and Dad don't want Charlie and me on different teams."

"Too much driving?" guesses Gray. "My folks are always complaining about the driving."

Kali tosses her thick braid over her shoulder. "Too much hockey. Period."

Whoa. Is it possible my parents aren't the only ones who think hockey is a waste of time?

"If I could play on the Wildcats, I would," says Charlie.

This earns Charlie a laugh from everyone but Kali. I chuckle along with my teammates. I'm feeling a bit more relaxed now as I secure my last buckle and pull out my granola bar.

"Shut it!" Kali jumps to her feet. "I need to tell you what Jas told me about the Bruins. Grand Forks has this new kid. Cane Johnson."

The dressing room goes quiet. She's got everyone's attention now. We know we can beat the Bruins. But there's no denying they're good. And they're probably going to be out for blood after losing against us last time. No one on our team's forgotten about that no-goal call, so I'm sure the Bruins haven't, especially since it cost them the game.

"He's good?" asks Jerry-Horn.

Kali nods. "He should be playing rep but he missed the tryouts, so they put him on the house team. His family just moved to BC."

Kali's not leaving any space between her words. With my mask on, I almost don't catch what she's saying. But I can tell by the way everyone's looking at me that this new guy's going to test me in a way I haven't been tested before.

"Cane Johnson," Charlie says, like he's adding it to the roster of players he keeps track of in his head.

"According to Jas, they call him Hurricane."

"Because he's always got gas?" asks Fartsby as he drops another bomb.

Dyne makes a loud farting noise with his lips that echoes Fartsby's explosion. Everyone laughs.

"No," Kali says when things finally settle down. "Because, just like the storm, he keeps coming. It's like nothing can stop him."

CHAPTER 21

All three periods of the game against the Bruins are boring. I'm talking snoozefest. For the first fifty minutes no one scores. Not even Cane. It's like everyone's waiting for a storm that never comes.

This is the finals—we're supposed to be at the top of our game. Instead it's like we've forgotten how to play. Passes are sloppy. Shots are weak. Skating is slow.

Maybe everyone's worn out from all the games we've already played this weekend. I sure am. My thigh muscles scream at me every time I crouch down. And my arms feel like they're made of rubber that's been stretched too far.

I ignore the pain and force myself to concentrate on the last ten minutes of the game. All I need to do is make one save at a time. But it's hard to concentrate when so much of the play is in the neutral zone.

As the time winds down and the score is still knotted at zero, I start wondering what happens next. Every tournament's different, but gold-medal games don't usually end in a tie. Sometimes there's overtime. Sometimes there's a shoot-out. Sometimes there's both.

No one on the ice knows the rules for this tournament until the horn finally blows. We skate over to the bench. Coach Matt tells us to line up for a shoot-out. "You know the drill. We each get three penalty shots. The team with the most goals wins the game," he says.

"And the tournament," Coach Lisa adds.

"Right," says Coach Matt. "Since we have more penalty minutes than the Bruins, we shoot first. We alternate from there. Any questions?"

"What if it's still tied after three?" asks Dyne.

"Then we shoot more." Jerry-Horn bumps his gloves together. "And it's sudden death."

My mouth—already parched from three periods in net—gets drier than the desert. In a drought. Shoot-outs are a goalie's worst nightmare.

"Not really," says Charlie. "Each team gets the same number of chances to score no matter how many shots we take."

I think about the replays I've seen of some truly epic shoot-outs. In the ones that get the most views on YouTube, it's always the last shot that decides the game. It might not be called sudden death, but it might as well be.

"Whatever. You know what I mean," says Jerry-Horn. "Why's everyone looking so serious? This is what we've been practicing for!"

While Coach Lisa figures out who our three shooters will be, Coach Tibor pulls me aside and tells me how to position myself. I'm trying to listen, but the diesel smell of the Zamboni is making me light-headed.

When I stepped up to be goalie, I never imagined this kind of pressure. How am I going to survive all these one-on-one matchups? Especially the one against Cane, who's probably been waiting the whole tournament for a moment like this. I have a horrible feeling he's about to go full cyclone.

Jerry-Horn gathers us into a huddle. "BLAZERS ON THREE!" he yells into the middle of our tight circle.

"One, two, three…Blazers!"

When the cheer's over, I know I have to leave the safety of my team and skate to the goal. But my skate blades feel like they're frozen to the ice. Duncan hands me my water bottle and slaps me on the back. Somehow I get my legs moving and skate to the crease without falling over.

I stand there. Alone.

We're shooting first, which is the only reason I'm still breathing. Going first is normally considered a disadvantage. In this case I'm glad it's the Bruins goalie—not me—who has to face the first shot.

Coach Matt sends Kali out on the ice. The whistle blows to start the shoot-out. A hush falls over the crowd as the ref drops the puck.

Kali circles once, then takes it up the middle. It looks like she's going to shoot straight at the goalie's pads, but at the last second she dangles and goes upstairs. The Bruins goalie flings his catcher's mitt up and makes the catch.

A golden opportunity from our best player. Denied.

SHOOT-OUT	1	2	3
TRAIL	X	O	O
GR.FORKS	O	O	O

I'm worried the Bruins will unleash the Hurricane for their first shot. For some reason, they don't. Maybe they're saving the best for last, but the player who comes off the bench instead looks just as intimidating. Then again, I'm nervous enough to be intimidated by a fly.

Trembling, I hit my blocker three times and tap each goal-post. The ref blows the whistle. As I crouch into position, my heart beats so fast I can hear the blood rushing past my ears.

Why did I wish for Carey Price to back off on the shut-outs? Right now I really need to be able to shut them out, one player at a time.

The Bruins player takes the puck from the center line and charges toward me. I come out of the crease—just a little—so it looks like I'm challenging him. A few strides away from the net he shifts to his back leg and fakes a shot. I go down, stacking my pads. The entire top of the net is open, but I can't do anything about it. And he can't lift the puck. No goal.

SHOOT-OUT	1	2	3
TRAIL	X	O	O
GR.FORKS	X	O	O

Seven's next for the Blazers. He glides forward and stops in the face-off circle. With a huge windup, he fakes a shot. It doesn't fool the goalie, who stands tall. Seven charges the crease, but he's in too deep and can't get a shot away.

SHOOT-OUT	1	2	3
TRAIL	X	X	O
GR. FORKS	X	O	O

The second shooter for the Bruins—still not Hurricane—skates in on my right. I go left because I can tell by her body position that she's going to cross over. She does. And when she shoots the puck, I'm there to stop it.

SHOOT-OUT	1	2	3
TRAIL	X	X	O
GR. FORKS	X	X	O

After four shooters, two for each side, I feel like I've been on the ice for a million years. I'm drowning in sweat, but somehow my sore body keeps moving as one shooter after another comes at me.

The shoot-out doesn't end at three. Because no one scores. Not Dyne, Jerry-Horn, Duncan, Gray, Madder, Fartsby… And not a single puck goes in the net behind me.

As the eighth shooter for the Bruins comes out onto the ice, I'm sure this is the one that's going to end my shutout.

"GO, JELLY!!" scream my teammates and coaches. From the stands I hear cheers for Elliot and the Blazers, mixed with cheers for the Bruins. My ears burn.

The player comes at me from a sharp angle. I hug the post and try to cover as much of the net as I can. Stickhandling, he comes closer and closer. I'm expecting the shot any second, but then he cuts across the crease to the side I've left wide open.

This is it. Game over.

The ref blows the whistle. I look behind me. The shot's gone wide. "No goal!" he shouts.

SHOOT-OUT	1	2	3	4	5	6	7	8
TRAIL	X	X	X	X	X	X	X	
GR. FORKS	X	X	X	X	X	X	X	

A mixture of relief and disbelief runs through me as I watch the ref grab the puck from the boards and skate to our bench. The other ref goes to the Bruins bench. They're each talking to the coaches about something.

I have no idea what I'm supposed to do. So when I see the Bruins goalie skate to his bench, I do the same.

"What's going on?" I whisper to Duncan, who looks like he's trying to overhear what they're saying.

"Sounds like we're running out of time," says Duncan. "And shooters."

I look down the bench. "There's still some people who haven't gone."

"The ones who haven't taken a shot don't want to," Duncan replies.

"Listen up, Blazers!" Coach Matt waves us into a huddle as the ref skates away. "One more shooter per side. If no one scores—or both players score—the game ends in a tie."

Kali's hand flies up in the air. "Pick me!"

"It's got to be someone who hasn't already taken a shot," says Coach Lisa.

We all look at each other. I flash back to the beginning of the season and the silence in the dressing room when Coach Matt was looking for someone to take Hunter's place. Despite the pressure of being in net—especially during a shoot-out—I'm glad I stepped up. Otherwise I'd be one of the players hiding on the bench right now because I didn't want to take a penalty shot.

A quiet voice breaks the tension. "I'll do it." It's Mouse.

"Okay, Nico, you got this," says Coach Tibor. "And Elliot"— Coach Tibor gives me a tap me on the shoulder pad— "remember to focus. Just one more save. You're doing great!"

I can't tell who's more nervous as Mouse and I skate away from the bench. He goes to center, and I go to the net. I wish I could stay at the bench to watch Mouse take his shot. The angle would be better, and I could cheer with my team. But the refs want both goalies in position for every shot, even though one of us isn't doing anything.

When the ref blows the whistle and drops the puck, Mouse pushes it forward rather than stickhandling. Then he skates to catch up. When he gets to the puck, he has no time to fake or deke or dangle. All he can do is take a weak shot right on net. The puck hits the goalie's blocker...trickles toward the post...bounces...and...

CHAPTER 22

I don't see what happens next. But I hear it. Blazers parents cheer and clap in unison. Mrs. Escobar's voice rises above everything. "THAT'S MY BOY!"

The ref points to the net, confirming the puck's over the line. "GOAL!"

SHOOT-OUT	1	2	3	4	5	6	7	8	9
TRAIL	X	X	X	X	X	X	X	✓	
GR. FORKS	X	X	X	X	X	X	X	O	

The Blazers bang their sticks against the boards. Cowbells and air horns scream their approval from our side of the arena.

Mouse almost trips as he flies to the bench. He skates past everyone, giving out fist bumps.

He's glowing like a nuclear reactor. I'm so happy Mouse gets to have this moment. I know—more than anyone—what it's like to feel you're not good enough.

But this marathon of a game isn't over yet.

I've pretty much forgotten about Hurricane until I hear one of the Bruins shout his name. He jumps out of the gate like something's been holding him back.

Great. It all comes down to me and him. If he scores, the game ends in a tie. If I can keep it out of the net, the Blazers win. After Mouse's heroic effort, we deserve—no, we *need*—the win.

Please Carey Price, I silently beg, *don't let me down now*.

The referee blows the whistle. I do my taps—blocker, blocker, blocker, post, post—and crouch into position, my eyes locked on Hurricane as he takes the puck. I've never been so determined in my life. I will stop this puck from going in the net if it's the last thing I do.

Instead of coming in deep, Hurricane takes a couple of strides over the blue line and stops. He looks a bit unsteady, and I wonder if he's injured. Maybe that's why they didn't play him earlier.

Which means I might actually have a chance. But as he gets closer, the butterflies in my stomach turn into bees. Angry bees.

Hurricane winds up. I assume it's a fake, so I stay on my feet. Still as a statue, I try to anticipate his next move.

His stick slaps the ice. Before I can react, the puck hits my stomach like a thousand-pound wrecking ball.

Doubled over in pain, I see the puck drop to the ice in front of me.

Hurricane charges toward it. With the end of his stick, he nudges it away from my leg pads.

I drop to my knees and dive for the puck. It skitters away from my blocker.

Just as it's about to slide out of reach, I lunge forward. Before Hurricane's stick can get there, I nab the puck with my catching glove. I squeeze my eyes shut and smother the puck with my entire body.

The whistle blows.

I almost can't hear it over the noise of the crowd. Everyone's on their feet at the bench.

The ref leans in close enough for me to smell his breath.

"You got the puck, kid?"

I reach underneath my equipment and pull out the puck. When I hand it to him, he raises it above his head and skates away, calling, "NO GOAL!"

SHOOT-OUT	1	2	3	4	5	6	7	8	9
TRAIL	X	X	X	X	X	X	X	✓	
GR.FORKS	X	X	X	X	X	X	X	X	

I skate toward the bench in a daze of disbelief. My teammates meet me mid-ice.

We throw our sticks and gloves in the air. Coach Matt doesn't let us carry on for too long, though. We need to shake hands and get our medals so we can clear the ice. The Zamboni's been waiting since the shoot-out began, which is practically a lifetime ago.

As the coaches line up to present Player of the Game, I wonder for a brief moment if it could be me. I immediately set the thought aside, because of course, it is Mouse who deserves it. And he gets it.

My teammates whistle and cheer for Mouse as he collects his prize. I clap along with them, super excited for Mouse and anxious to collect our gold medals so we can get off the ice. I want to continue the celebration in the dressing room, where we don't have to worry about hurting the other team's feelings. I can tell by the look on their faces that they're not at all happy with winning silver.

"And since this is the last game, I now get the pleasure of announcing Player of the Tournament," the Bruins coach says.

Wait. What?

I hear the words, but there's no time to process what's happening.

"Player of the Tournament is Elliot Feldner-Martel!"

I'm practically floating as we collect our medals. Even though I got a shutout in every game, I can't believe I won Player of the Tournament. Going from the worst kid on the ice to the best is not something that happens to people like me. This is the stuff that only happens in stories.

Heading off the ice, I hear someone call my name. "Elliot?" he repeats.

I turn. It's Hurricane. He smiles. "You're good. Ever thought about playing rep?"

It's the last thing I expect to hear from someone with the nickname Hurricane. From anyone, for that matter. I look behind me, sure he must be talking to Duncan.

Hurricane fist-bumps my glove. "I can't believe you stopped all those shots!"

"Your goalie was good too," I say. "And so were you."

"It was fun. Congrats," he says before skating past me.

Instead of feeling good, I suddenly feel like a fraud. I can't believe Hurricane thinks I should play rep. What would he say if he knew I was getting help from a hunk of plastic molded into the shape of Carey Price?

I try not to think about it so I can enjoy the postgame celebration in the dressing room. It's not hard. These are the moments that made me want to be part of the team and not just an ornament on the bench—a player who actually helped my team win.

"Mouse! Hero of the game!" Duncan says as we shower him with water from our bottles.

Jerry-Horn blasts our win song through his Bluetooth speakers. I'm singing into the butt end of Charlie's stick, which is doubling as a microphone, when I hear Hunter behind me.

"Good news, Blazers! My physio thinks I'll be ready to play in the new year."

This is the first time Hunter's talked about getting back on the ice since he hurt his knee. Why would he bring it up now?

I swallow back a puck-sized lump of phlegm. January's just over five weeks away.

"What if we don't need you anymore?" asks Charlie. "You gonna play out?"

Hunter's face puffs up as his neck turns red. Either the collar of his shirt's too tight or this trash talk's actually getting to him. "I've never played out. I've been in goal full-time for more than three seasons."

"Well, it's going to be pretty hard to get Jelly out of net with all the goose eggs he's been collecting," says Jerry-Horn.

The thought that I could permanently replace Hunter doesn't make me feel good. Instead it makes me scared. Because I know the truth. Despite everything—the shutouts, the gold medal, the Player of the Tournament—I'm really not as good as everyone thinks I am.

CHAPTER 23

I plan to arrive early for our next two practices, hoping to get some extra skating practice. It works on Tuesday because the ice is clear and Coach Tibor's early too. It doesn't work on Wednesday. But at least I'm dressed and ready to go as soon as the gate opens.

After school, Duncan tells me he can't play mini sticks because Hunter's coming over. He doesn't tell me why Hunter's coming over, and I don't ask. Well, I try to ask, but the words get stuck. I can't remember the last time Duncan and I didn't hang out after school. And now he's hanging out with Hunter of all people.

I know I should catch up on homework. First, I need to burn off some of this negative energy. After going through my regular dryland routine, I still want more exercise. I search for goalie exercises online and do as many as I can find.

Still not ready to tackle my homework, I fiddle with my toaster invention until I finally get it working. Sort of. It doesn't fire pucks, but I figure out how to get it to shoot cardboard discs (before they burn). If I stand close enough, my reflexes get a pretty good workout. It takes me a while to get through all the drills I've set up for myself, though—which doesn't leave much time for homework.

I know this is bad. But I'm not too worried about it until the next day when Mr. Morrisette announces there's going to be a math quiz on Friday. Then I panic.

Instead of going to the public skate Thursday night after dinner, I sit at my desk, unwrap a piece of spearmint gum and force myself to open my textbook. Chewing gum while studying isn't just a silly superstition—according to all those books Mom reads, it's supposed to help me think.

It doesn't work. My mind keeps wandering ahead to our game against the Wildcats this weekend. I want to play well and help my team win, so I need help from Carey Price. But if I get another shutout, people are going to get suspicious. They probably already are. No goalie in the history of the world has ever had a shutout in every game.

Besides, I never wanted to be a hockey star. I just wanted to be good enough to fit in on the team.

It's suddenly clear to me what I really want—and what I don't.

"Okay, Pricer." I pick up the bobblehead. "I don't want a shutout in every game. I just want to be able to skate as well as my teammates. And I want to be a decent goalie."

Carey Price's plastic lips stay fixed in a smile that suddenly looks like a smirk. I shake the doll. Where's the magic coming from, anyway? It's one thing to be superstitious. But do I actually think this bobblehead can grant whatever wish I make?

It doesn't seem possible. But how else could I have gotten all those shutouts?

"Okay…" I say slowly. "I have another wish. How about a good grade in math?"

When the quiz lands on my desk the next morning, I stare at the empty space between the questions. None of it makes any sense. And it's not even multiple choice.

Doodling in the corners of the test page, I wait for the magic to hit my pencil the way it hit my goalie stick. I steal a glance at Aislyn. She's practically bouncing in her seat. Next to her, Duncan sits as straight as a ruler. Both are writing furiously.

A wave of exhaustion hits me. I put my head down on the desk and close my eyes. Blobs that look like the Carey Price bobblehead appear behind my eyelids. "Zero's a good score for a goalie," he says, "not for a math test."

I bolt upright in my chair. Did I fall asleep? Or was I hearing voices?

All the blank space between the questions is still blank, except for a small patch of drool that's soaked through the paper. This is not turning out the way I expected. Then again, I still have no idea what to expect.

My forehead breaks out in a sweat as my heart rate picks up. Every muscle in my body contracts, and I jump up from my desk.

Grabbing the quiz, I crumple it in my fist. On the way out the door, I hurl the ball of paper in the trash.

Mr. Morrisette calls after me. I ignore him and race down the hallway to the bathroom and lock myself in the stall.

I stay there until the bell rings. When the next bell rings to start English, I know I have to do something. I just don't know what. I can't show my face after losing it in class. But it's not like I can sneak out of school for the rest of the day either. If I do that, the principal will call home. For sure.

After lots of deep breathing (not a pleasant thing to do in the bathroom), I decide to go to English and pretend nothing happened. I get weird looks from the kids who are in both my math and English class—including Duncan—but as Ms. Deadmarsh starts explaining today's assignment, my classmates forget about me.

I am starting to think I've gotten away with it when Mr. Morrisette appears at the door near the end of class and asks to see me. "Do we need to set up another meeting with Ms. Kuhn and your parents?"

I force myself to look him in the eye. "Can you give me a little more time to catch up on my work? Please?"

After a few seconds of silence—that feels more like a few centuries—he exhales. "Fine. But you need to get your parents to sign this and bring it back to me on Monday."

He hands me my crumpled-up quiz. I want to snatch it out of his hands and rip it to shreds. Instead I plaster a smile on my face, take the quiz and count to ten as fast as I can. "Will do."

CHAPTER 24

I arrive at the rink on Saturday with a plan. The wish I made to get a good math grade didn't work, so the wish to get a shutout in every game must be nonsense too. And I am going to prove it—by letting in a goal.

I get ready quickly, anxious to put my plan to the test. I'm already eating my granola bar when Hunter walks into the dressing room. I actually smell him before I see him. Nothing stands out more in a room full of stale sweat mixed with the stink of Gray's socks than pine-scented deodorant.

"Ready for another blowout, Blazers?" he asks.

"What makes you think it's going to be a blowout?" Kali lets the door fall closed behind her with a bang.

"Because we're playing the Wildcats." Hunter plugs his nose. "They're all girls," he says in a high-pitched voice.

I stop chewing and scan the room. Does everyone else think Hunter's totally out of line?

"The Wildcats are good," says Charlie. "They won the BC U13 Female Hockey Championships last year. And their coach used to play for Team Canada."

"Yeah, you big Neanderthal." Kali swings her helmet at Hunter. She does it playfully, but I can tell she's irritated. I don't blame her. "The Wildcats have some awesome players. Including Jas, their goalie. She has some awesome moves. We're all in trouble if we think it's going to be easy to beat her."

I remember Jas—she's the one who warned Kali about Cane. I wonder if she knows that Kali's now warning us about her.

"Oh yeah," says Dyne, "Jas was in one of my hockey camps this summer. She's really good."

"Maybe for a girl," says Hunter. "But I still think we're going to destroy them."

I clench my fists. Hunter being a jerk is nothing new. But I can't believe he's saying these things in front of Kali. I can't believe he thinks they're true.

I want to say a million things at once. But I can't get the words out in time.

"Don't be a jerk." Kali's braid swings beneath her helmet as she snaps it into place. Turning away from Hunter, she addresses the rest of us. "When we're on the ice, everyone's the same."

I try to remember Kali's words as I wait at the gate with my teammates. Truthfully, though, talk of how good Jas is has made me nervous. And if the rest of the Wildcats are as good as Kali, we're in serious trouble.

Catching a glimpse of Jas during warm-up, I decide that it doesn't really matter. We're first in our division. We can afford to lose a game. And after the stupid stuff Hunter said, I kind of want the girls to win.

I'm ready to let in a goal. Maybe more.

The Wildcats win the face-off. Right away they're storming the net. Without thinking, I move into position to make one save. Then another. And another.

When Seven finally intercepts and sends the puck down the ice for a dump and chase, I realize it would've been easy to let in one of those rebounds. But it's early. And I don't want to make it too obvious that I'm trying to let them score.

Besides, I don't want the Wildcats to get ahead of us by too much. Carey Price doesn't seem to be granting wishes, so he might not be lucky anymore either. Still, I'm glad I had the usual pre-game chat with him before coming to the rink.

I play on instinct for the rest of the first. I keep expecting them to score on me, but somehow the puck stays out of the net. Before I know it twenty minutes has passed, and neither team has a goal.

During the break between periods, I don't hear anything the coaches say. I'm too busy trying to figure out how to make my plan work. I didn't think I'd have to work to *not* make a save.

We get three goals past Jas in the second. The Wildcats don't score, though, despite a bunch of good chances. With less than a minute left in the period, a Wildcat forward steals the puck from Jerry-Horn at the blue line and charges toward me on a breakaway.

This is it.

She comes in on the right, so I go left. Instead of shooting at the open side, she cuts to the middle. I can tell she's going to lift the puck, so I go down. It's a good shot, and I'm sure she's going to roof it. The puck grazes my shoulder pad. I try to duck under it, but that just pushes the puck forward. I leave the rebound there for the Wildcat center who's at the front of net. She gets a stick on it but hits the post.

It's like there's something blocking my net. And it's not me.

The third period starts. I don't hit my blocker three times. I don't tap my goalposts. This is not the time for superstition or luck. This is the time to let in a goal. Now or never.

I'm on edge the entire period, expecting the puck to slide across the line behind me. It doesn't. Time is running out, and I have no idea what to do. I can't just lie down and let them shoot over me. But I'm so desperate that at one point I even close my eyes.

The goal never comes. Final score, 3–0 Blazers.

CHAPTER 25

I rush to the dressing room. I don't want anyone to see how badly I'm shaken.

I got to the arena wanting to let in a goal. After what Hunter said in the dressing room, I went into the game wanting the Wildcats to win. But I couldn't make either one happen. It's like the shutout wish has become a shutout curse.

"I never thought I'd say this, but these shutouts are getting kind of boring." Madder drops his stick into the corner of the dressing room behind the door and collapses on the bench next to me.

Hunter has followed him into the dressing room. "Boring? That game was a total joke."

"I told you they were good," says Charlie.

Madder nods. "You weren't wrong!"

"They weren't that good." Hunter's still standing in the middle of the room. "You guys were that bad. You couldn't even find the net!"

I try to remind myself that trash-talking is part of the game. But I'm already upset, and Hunter's making it worse. "At least we won."

"Ha! You call that a win?"

Seven rolls his eyes. "I guess you think we'll have more blowouts when you're back?"

"Are you kidding?" Hunter shakes his head. "You must have the memory of a goldfish cracker. Jelly couldn't even skate last year. Once he's playing out, he'll bring us all down."

My chest tightens. My emotions get the better of me at home sometimes. But I never get angry in front of my friends.

1, Goldfish crackers, 2, Sour Patch Kids, 3, Gummi Bears, 4, Gummi Worms, 5, Gummi—

"Whoa. Time to back off, Hunter," says Gray.

"You're just anxious because you want to play," adds Duncan. "Don't take it out on Elliot."

I'm glad my friends are sticking up for me. But I still want to rip my leg pad in two.

"I'll be back on the ice any day now. Just waiting for a final approval from my physio," says Hunter.

Any day?

"It'll be good to have you back," says Jerry-Horn. "Jelly's gotten a lot better and—"

Hunter cuts in. "Doesn't anyone wonder how he's done it? Seems like more than a bit of puck luck to me."

Even though I knew this was coming, something inside me snaps. "What would you know about puck luck? You're the unluckiest thing that's ever happened to this team. If it weren't for me, the Blazers would be without a goalie. All because you got yourself hurt—probably showing off on the trampoline or something. But you know what? As long as you're on the bench, you should just shut up already!"

When I finally stop talking, the dressing room is eerily quiet. Duncan shoots me a worried look. My heart stops racing, and I know I've gone too far. But Hunter should've listened when Gray told him to back off.

"Who do you think—"

The dressing-room door swings open, and Hunter stops abruptly. It's his dad. "What's taking so long? You guys have to clear the room for the next team!"

There's a moment of pause before everyone rushes to pack away the last of their equipment.

"Let's go, Hunter," his dad says over the noise. "We need to get to physio. You're not getting any better hanging around with this team."

A shiver runs down my spine. Hunter's dad gives me the creeps. I don't know what he meant when he said Hunter wasn't getting any better hanging around with us. It was an insult, that much I know for sure.

Instead of feeling insulted, though, I feel a bit sorry for Hunter. Not enough to forgive him for what he said. But enough to make me wish I hadn't let my mouth run wild.

As much as I don't like Hunter, I don't want him for an enemy. With so much weird stuff going on, that's the very last thing I need.

CHAPTER 26

That night all the Blazers go to the Smoke Eaters game to celebrate Madder's birthday. Sitting in the stands with them—as far away from Hunter as possible—I try to forget about the tension in the dressing room. I know I should apologize for telling him to shut up. I'm still upset about the things he said, though. Not just about me but about the girls as well.

Still, I don't want anything to wreck the fun of being at the game with my team. This is exactly the kind of thing I dreamed of doing when I wasn't allowed to play.

During the first period, we all sit together in the very front row. Every time a Smokies player bumps up against the boards, we pound our fists on the glass. Dyne gets popcorn, and soon it's flying everywhere as we try to toss kernels into each other's gaping mouths.

The silliness stops when Jerry-Horn spots some Wildcats players during first intermission. "Look, it's Jas and her friends," he says as he points toward the mezzanine.

"Does anyone else think Jas is kind of cute?" asks Gray.

This catches me off guard. I'd much rather talk about hockey, but I have to admit, the girls do look a lot different without all their gear on. Different in a good way, although I'd never admit it. Gray sure was brave.

"Is that why you didn't want us to beat them too badly today?" asks Hunter. "Because you didn't want to hurt your girlfriend's feelings?"

"She's not my girlfriend." Gray grabs Hunter's toque. Next thing you know, we're all playing catch with it, and Jerry-Horn's providing the commentary. At one point we almost lose it over the glass.

The teams come back on the ice. Thirty-three seconds into the second period the Smokies score. We go ballistic. Charlie rings his mom's cowbell, and the oversize black-and-orange Smoke Eaters foam hands Mouse brought turn into swords.

And once again Hunter gets away with being Hunter.

As the second period comes to an end, Jas shows up in the aisle beside our seats. Three other Wildcats players are with her.

"Whatcha guys doing?" asks one of the girls I don't know.

"Hitchhiking to Hong Kong." Hunter sticks his thumb in the air. "What does it look like we're doing?"

Everyone laughs, though I'm sure I'm not the only one who doesn't get the joke. Charlie scratches his head. "Don't you need a boat to get to Hong Kong?"

Before anyone can answer, Jerry-Horn does a loud, dramatic sniff. "Pe-ew! Who cut the cheese?"

Fartsby's face turns red. "Excuse me."

Now everyone laughs like they mean it—including Fartsby.

"Good game," Mouse says, nodding toward the empty ice.

Two of the girls speak at once. "Great game!"

"A lot better than the game we played today," says Hunter.

Oh no. Here we go again. My shoulders stiffen in anticipation. I'm sure he's still mad about the things I said. I bet he'll do anything to get in the last word, especially now that he's got a bigger audience.

I turn away from him and accidentally make eye contact with the girl standing next to Jas. "You played well," she says.

I feel a blush light up my cheeks. "Um, thanks…" I try to guess what number she is so I can compliment her back, but I'm not quick enough.

"Jelly here eats more Lucky Charms than anyone I know." Hunter's at the other end of the row, but I can hear him clearly even with my back turned.

Even though he's not saying anything new, this comment stings like never before. I stare at a piece of bubblegum stuck to the back of the chair in front of me and try not to let it show.

"Lucky Charms! Yum!" Dyne rubs his belly. "Anyone want to hit the concession again?"

Jas nods. "We're heading there anyway."

"I'll guard the seats," I say. The arena's not exactly packed, but I need a break from the trash talk.

"I'll stay too," says Duncan. Everyone else jumps out of their seats.

"You okay?" he asks me when they're gone.

"Sure." I chew at a loose piece of skin around my fingernail. "Hunter just gets to me sometimes."

Duncan stares at the ice even though there's nothing to see. I watch as a couple of rink attendants shovel snow from the corners. For once I have no idea what Duncan's thinking. Should I say something about what happened in the dressing room?

"Hunter's a bit much," Duncan finally says. "But he's got a lot going on."

I can't believe Duncan's defending Hunter. "I've got a lot going on too," I blurt out.

"Like what?"

Duncan looks like he really wants to know. And that he really cares.

All my insecurities come gushing toward me like a dam just broke or something. Next thing I know, I'm telling him all about the wishes I made on the Carey Price bobblehead.

"You should get rid of it," Duncan says when I'm finished.

I had my fingers crossed the whole time I was talking, hoping Duncan would react the way Grandpa did when I told him about the magic. I uncross them with a sigh of relief. "But what if I start losing?"

"Do you really think it's magic? I mean, it didn't help you with your math test, did it?"

"But if it's not magic, how did I get that shutout today?"

"I don't know. Maybe you're actually good?"

144

Before I can react—or even figure out how to react—the gang all returns. They're laughing and pointing at the screen. It's the kiss cam. And it's aimed right at us.

Jerry-Horn bends down and gives Duncan a kiss on the cheek.

Everyone hoots and cheers. There are shoulder punches and hand slaps as everyone tries to attract enough attention to keep the camera focused on us.

I try to laugh along. But all I can think about is how to get the focus off me. I shudder, thinking of what would happen if everyone found out about my bobblehead.

"Please don't tell anyone what I told you," I say to Duncan as our teammates fill the seats around us.

"I won't," he says.

CHAPTER 27

When I wake up Sunday morning, the house is quiet. According to the calendar, Dad's taken Aislyn to some robotics thing and Mom's campaigning.

After gobbling down a banana I barely even taste, I head back to my room. I'm greeted by the pile of homework that's been sitting on my desk since the meeting with Ms. Kuhn. I kept expecting Dad to bug me about it, but he never did. Because he trusted me, I guess.

I did promise I'd try to do better at school. And I feel pretty bad that I didn't follow through.

I pull the crumpled-up quiz out of my backpack. When I ask my parents to sign it, all my school struggles are going to come charging back into the spotlight. Whether I ask Mom or Dad will make no difference—both will turn it into a big deal. The only way I'm going to survive is by showing them that I've at least tried to catch up.

I stuff a piece of gum in my mouth and set one of the worksheets in front of me. I sharpen my pencil. I want to do the work. But I don't know where to start.

My knees bob up and down under my desk. I just need to work off some of this energy. Then I'll be able to concentrate.

I look at my toaster invention, and I get an idea. Mom has a plug-in pencil sharpener downstairs. I wonder if I can get it to shoot something at me super fast, in random directions.

I can't find the electric pencil sharpener, so instead I pick up the laptop and take it back to my room. It's been a while since I called Grandpa. I'm not sure he can help me with my homework, but talking to him always makes me feel better. Besides I need to thank him for the Fred Sasakamoose book. Grandpa's sent me lots of hockey books but this is the first one that's actually written for adults. It made me feel quite grown up—even if Grandpa did suggest that I read it with Mom.

I press on his icon and wait for him to answer. When the webcam opens on the laptop, though, it's Grandma sitting on the other end.

We talk for a while about nothing, really, and then I ask to talk to Grandpa.

"He's not feeling so well, Elliot."

"Does he have a cold?"

Grandma frowns. "Something like that."

I'm confused. Grandpa's been sick before, but I don't ever remember him being too sick to talk to me. "Can I talk to him later?"

Grandma shakes her head and says something about the time change. Quebec's three hours ahead, so they've probably eaten dinner. Does that mean he's already in bed? Before I can ask, Grandma says goodbye.

A few hours later I hear the van pull into the driveway. Guilt spears me like a hockey stick. I haven't gotten any schoolwork done. I tried everything I could think of to help me concentrate—fitness training, goalie drills, video games, YouTube—but every time I sat down at my desk, I was distracted again.

If only I could go back and do everything all over. Not just back to the beginning of the day but to the beginning of the school year. Or at least the beginning of the hockey season. I stop pacing in front of my dresser and stare at Carey Price.

"Let's be clear." I pick up the bobblehead to make sure I've got his attention. "First I wanted a win. Then I wanted a shutout. Then a shutout in every game. It turns out that was a mistake. No more shutouts! My wish is just to be good enough to fit in on the team. And as for math—"

"Are you talking to your bobblehead doll?"

I spin around. My sister is standing just outside my bedroom door.

"It's not a doll." My cheeks flush as I drop Carey Price into the trash can next to my desk.

Aislyn taps a finger against her chin. "Sounds to me like you *were* talking to it. And maybe even making a wish?"

"It's *not* a doll!"

Aislyn grins. "Do you think your bobblehead is some kind of genie?"

"No! If I did, would I have thrown it in the garbage?"

Ignoring my protests, Aislyn adds, "You know that genies only grant three wishes, right?"

Her words hit me like a wrecking ball. *Only three.* Maybe that's what's wrong! What if I'm out of wishes?

I need to think. But Aislyn's still talking about magic and genies and stuff.

"Don't you have something better to do?" My throat itches. I cover my face with my hand, worried that I might actually start to cry.

"I do have to work on my project. The wind turbine—"

"I don't care!" My head is pounding. "Please just get out of my room."

My sister stares at me for a second before turning to leave. I make sure the door is completely closed before collapsing into my desk chair.

What if Aislyn's right and I only get three wishes? Will I be stuck getting shutouts for the rest of my life? Or worse— will I be on my own when Hunter comes back and I'm forced to play out? Without any more wishes, will I go back to being the worst player on the ice?

My problems are piling up even more than my stack of unfinished homework. I glance at my desk. The crumpled-up quiz is sitting there, unsigned.

I think back to the list of conditions I agreed to in order for Dad to let me play hockey. I was surprised when he didn't kick me off the team after the first meeting with Ms. Kuhn. There's no way I'm getting away with it again. And even though everything's totally messed up, I can't become an *un*-Blazer. Not after all the work I've done to become part of the team.

There's only one way out of this mess. Heart thumping like Harvey the Hound pounding a drum at a Flames game, I pick up a pen and sign Dad's name on the bottom of the quiz.

CHAPTER 28

The week whizzes by faster than you can say *Fred "Chief Running Deer" Sasakamoose*. I have to get ready for another game tomorrow.

FRED SASAKAMOOSE
CHIEF RUNNING DEER
Chicago Black Hawks
Center

21

FIRST INDIGENOUS PLAYER IN THE NHL
WITH TREATY STATUS

Before going to bed, I pack my hockey bag so I'm ready when Coach Matt picks me up in the morning. Hunter hasn't dressed for practice this week, so I assume he's not ready to play.

Still, I wonder if I should pack my non-goalie gear, just in case.

The thought of playing out of the net makes my stomach flip. But if Hunter was going to play goal for the Blazers tomorrow, Coach Matt or Coach Tibor would've told me. So I'm pretty sure I'm safe in net for at least one more game.

Safe in net. Am I really safe anywhere on the ice anymore?

I toss and turn in bed as different scenarios play out in my head.

If Aislyn's right, and I only get three wishes, I'll get another shutout tomorrow. If Duncan's right, and the bobble-head's not really magic, who knows what will happen. But if it *is* magical—or even just lucky—then my wish to be good enough to fit in should come true.

Could I actually just be good at hockey? No matter what position I play?

The bobblehead's still sitting at the bottom of the trash can next to my desk. Should I have my usual pre-game chat with him? Or is it time for me to cut back on the superstitions?

Grandpa told me once that athletes are superstitious because they want to believe they have some control over stuff that often comes down to chance—like having the puck bounce the right way. Even if it's not real, believing you have control can give you confidence.

Right now I could use some control. And a whole lot of confidence.

I glance at my clock. It's just past midnight—game day. Maybe if I talk to Carey Price for just a few minutes, I'll be able to sleep. And I won't have to fit something else into my routine tomorrow morning.

Whether I'm in net or out, I can't face the game tomorrow without my lucky bobblehead.

I creep out of bed, avoiding the creaking plank of wood in my floor. There's a little bit of light from the hallway shining through the crack under my door, which probably means Mom's working late. I don't want her to hear me, so I move with the stealth of a cat on the prowl as I tiptoe toward my desk.

I reach into the trash can.

The bobblehead is gone.

When my alarm goes off in the morning, I feel like I haven't slept at all. I had weird dreams all night.

In the one I remember most clearly, I was at the arena. I came out of the dressing room and in a moment of total panic realized I was wearing cowboy boots. As Coach Tibor pushed me onto the ice, I tried to say something about being out of wishes, but no words came out. It felt like my mouth had been taped shut. I tried to shake my head side to side to say "No" but for some reason I could only move my chin up and down.

I was still nodding like a bobblehead when I woke up. I haul my bag downstairs and head to the kitchen to grab some breakfast. Mom's already up and scrolling through something on her phone.

I want to ask if she knows anything about my bobblehead. I'm hoping she'll say she emptied my garbage can. I'd even be happy if she got mad at me for not doing it myself. But what if that's not the answer?

It doesn't look like Mom's had any more sleep than I did, so I decide not to bother her. Instead I gobble down my breakfast and give her a kiss on the cheek before saying goodbye.

"Good luck with the game, honey," she says.

I don't respond.

My knees bounce up and down like a jackhammer in the back seat of Coach Matt's car. Once again, I have questions. And once again, I'm afraid of the answers.

As we turn into the arena parking lot, I know I can't wait any longer. The suspense is killing me. "Is Hunter playing today?"

Coach Matt glances at me through the rearview mirror. "Not today."

I exhale a breath I didn't realize I'd been holding.

"He got the green light to play," he continues, "but his dad wants to wait."

"His dad doesn't want him to risk getting reinjured in a game that doesn't matter," Duncan adds.

"Oh," I say.

"You sound disappointed, Elliot." Coach Matt pulls into a parking spot and cuts the engine. "I should've checked in with you earlier." He swivels around to face me. "Do you need a break?"

To be honest, I have no idea what I need. And there's no time to think about it. "I'm good. But...thanks."

No one scores in the first two periods of our game against the Coyotes. Not us. Not them.

I assume—since the bobblehead's gone—that the Coyotes aren't scoring on me because they're not very good. They seem to be getting very frustrated, though. A lot of them are playing dirty—hitting me in the pads after the whistle's gone or giving me an extra shove when the ref's not looking—especially their biggest player, number 16.

"We've got to find more openings, Blazers," Coach Matt says at the end of the second. "Elliot can't hold them off forever."

I glance at Duncan, wondering what he's thinking. I haven't told him that I threw out the bobblehead like he suggested. Or that it's missing.

Duncan stares at the ice, silent. Like the rest of the Blazers.

Except Hunter. "You guys need to shoot the puck!" he yells at us from the bench.

"Really?" Jerry-Horn responds. "Jeez, I hadn't thought of that!"

My entire team seems on edge. Probably because it's so early. Still, I can't help thinking it has something to do with me and all these shutouts. It doesn't seem like anyone's looking me in the eye. Or congratulating me after a save. Or even joking around and trash-talking me like usual.

"Let's focus." Coach Lisa pulls out the little whiteboard and starts making marks with her dry-erase marker. "The Coyotes are weak on the left side, so let's try taking the puck in the zone like this…"

I don't usually pay attention to the plays Coach Lisa draws up. I know I should—especially now that I'm going to be forced out of the net—but I can't.

"Once we have control, the defense can move up a bit to add pressure."

The Coyotes coach must give his team the same advice. The instant the third period starts, they storm the net. Their first shot hits my mask so hard I actually see stars. Somehow, I still make the save.

Gray checks to see if I'm okay, then points at his helmet. "Good thing you're wearing your brain bucket, Jelly!"

Gray's support settles me down. A little.

The Coyotes win the draw and dump the puck deep into the Blazers' zone. Madder gets there first, takes control of the puck and banks it off the boards. The forwards chase after it. Jerry-Horn carries it down the middle. A few strides over the blue line, Jerry-Horn pulls the puck back to Kali, who elevates a wrister.

SCORE!

The Coyotes goalie whacks his stick against both posts. I feel the vibration all the way down at my end of the rink. The rest of his team's just as frustrated. They swarm the crease to get it back.

I get hammered from all sides, until I don't even know up from down anymore. The puck hits me. Sticks hit me. I get shoved from behind. I spin around and come face-to-face with number 16. "You suck, goalie," he sneers through his cage. "If your defense wasn't solid, we'd be crushing you."

The whistle blows, and the referee skates over to retrieve the puck. It's in my catching glove.

I have no idea how it got there even though my hand's still stinging from the impact.

Sixteen knocks me with his shoulder as he skates past. "You don't even know where the puck is…what a loser."

"Don't let him get to you," Duncan says as he crouches into position for the face-off.

I know he's right. But it's hard. There's always chatter between teams. Mostly single words—or a string of single words—that Dad would consider truck-driver language. But 16's using full sentences and hitting between the pads, right where it hurts most.

1, Carey Price, 2, Patrick Roy, 3, Martin Brodeur, 4, Curtis Joseph, 5, Dominik Hašek…

It seems like every time the puck's in our zone, 16's in the crease—my crease—blocking my view and poking me with his stick. After every whistle he chirps at me like a cockroach.

"One of your teammates said you were a total bender last year. How'd you go from a bender to a sieve?"

It's like I've been punched in the gut. I bend over, totally winded.

How can he call me a sieve when I haven't let in a single goal?

But that's not the part that gets to me most. The word that makes my intestines knot up is *bender*—someone who really sucks at hockey, a player whose ankles bend because they can't skate.

One of my teammates used that word to describe…me.

I'm too upset to remember any other of my favorite goalies, so I start over with something easier. *1, red, 2, yellow, 3, blue, 4, purple, 5, orange, 6, brown, 7, black…*

I can't get my heart rate under control, even when the play is in the other end. And it never takes long for the Coyotes to be back on the attack.

One of their defensemen rips a slap shot from the point. It misses by a mile—deflecting off the glass out of play—but I go down like a gun's been fired above my head.

Sixteen comes barreling toward me. He does a hockey stop in the crease, showering my mask with snow. "Your luck will run out eventually."

I'm suddenly hot enough to melt the entire slab of ice. I grab his leg and yank him down to the ice.

Then I hit him.

CHAPTER 29

I'm not sure what happens next. My head leaves my body. By the time it comes back, all three officials are at the net, trying to break up a crowd.

Madder, Dyne and two Coyotes get offsetting penalties for roughing. I get a double minor for instigating and roughing.

We can't play without a goalie, so Mouse has to kill my penalty. It might as well be me in the box. My body still feels detached from my head as I go through the motions of making each save. The Blazers are just as mad as the Coyotes now, and they totally shut them down. I say *they* because I don't feel like part of it. Even when the puck hits my pad or blocker.

By the time my penalty's over, there's only three minutes left in the game. The Coyotes pull their goalie, so we're short-handed again. Before they can even get a shot on net, Kali pockets an empty netter.

The game ends 2–0.

I skate slowly to our bench, totally out of breath. Everyone's excited—for different reasons. Coach Lisa thinks I gave our team the spark we needed. Coach Tibor is not happy about my penalty, but he's thrilled with the way we shut down their power play. Coach Matt says nothing.

On the way to the dressing room, Coach Matt pulls me aside.

As we wait for everyone else to file past us, the shame I'm feeling goes into overdrive. I don't know what to say or how to explain what happened out there. Nothing's going to change the fact that *hitting is not a good way of dealing with my problems.* Mom hasn't had to tell me that since preschool.

"I'm sorry, Coach Matt. I didn't mean to hit him. I just… my temper…"

He puts up his hand like a crossing guard waving a stop sign. "Can I ask you a question, Elliot?"

My stomach knots. "Uh, sure?" I say, because really, what choice do I have?

"Like I said in the car, I should've checked in with you earlier."

"Right, about being goalie and needing a break."

Coach nods. "Yeah, that. But also…are you having fun playing hockey this year?"

I look down at the wet hallway floor, unable to hold his gaze. I think about the fact that he drafted me to his team. About all the rides he's given me. I owe Duncan and his dad so much…of course I'm having fun. I'm playing hockey, right?

But for some reason, I can't say the words.

"Okay, another question," Coach Matt finally says. "Do you know why I picked you for my team?"

"Because my parents asked you to? Or maybe so you could give me rides?"

Coach Matt chuckles and shakes his head. "As much as I enjoy being a taxi driver, no. That's not the reason."

A rip of laughter escapes through the dressing-room door. I want to be in there. Not out here, staring at the floor.

I can tell Coach Matt isn't going to say anything else until I look up, so I force myself to lift my chin. He isn't smiling. But he isn't frowning either.

"It's because of your attitude," he continues. "You had the best attitude on the team last year. Every practice, every game, you were excited just by the idea of getting to play."

He pauses to give me a chance to reply. I don't.

"I wish that hadn't changed," he adds.

A lump the size of a Zamboni blocks my throat.

"It's like you've lost the love you had for the game."

I wait for him to say something about my shutouts. About the miraculous turnaround I've made since last season. From worst to first and all that.

He doesn't. Instead he claps me on the shoulder and opens the dressing-room door.

Our win song smacks me in the face like a cold gust of wind. Coach Matt doesn't follow me into the dressing room. I let the door swing closed behind me and then pause for a second before looking up to face my team.

No one pays any attention to me. In varying states of undress, they're too busy talking and laughing among themselves.

Fartsby and Charlie are playing keep-away with Gray's stinky socks. Jerry-Horn and Dyne are playing some game that involves knocking each other over while they're balanced on medicine balls. Seven and Madder pass a roll of tape back and forth with their sticks, knocking down everything in the way.

The Blazers are acting like it was just another game. I want to fool around with them—have some of that fun Coach Matt was talking about—but for me, it wasn't just another game.

I can't believe I hit number 16. He was annoying, sure, but he just put me over the edge. It was all my fears—of Hunter coming back, of continuing to get shutouts, of not being accepted by my teammates—that added up to something I just couldn't deal with anymore.

I drop onto an open spot on the bench, close to my bag. As I concentrate on getting out of my sweaty clothes, I wonder if anyone will say something about my penalty.

I've just managed to wrestle my way out of my leg pads when I hear Hunter behind me.

"This your doll, Jelly?"

I spin around. He's standing over my hockey bag.

Holding my Carey Price bobblehead.

CHAPTER 30

Jerry-Horn cuts the music.

"I don't know where that came from," I stammer. "I've never seen it before."

"Really?" Hunter glances at Duncan.

I want to rip Carey Price out of Hunter's grubby fingers. How did the bobblehead get into my hockey bag?

And why did I lie about it?

Just because it's in my bag doesn't mean it's magic. Or responsible for my shutouts.

Everyone in the room is watching Hunter and me. It's like there's a spotlight shining right in my eyes. I can't think. Especially because my brain is screaming, *How did Carey Price get into my hockey bag?*

Hunter's silent as he reads a piece of notepaper that looks like it's taped to the back of the bobblehead. I can't see what it says or find any clue to where the bobblehead came from.

Duncan throws stuff in his bag. "We should probably clear the room for the next game."

"You better put this somewhere safe, Jelly." Hunter holds up the bobblehead like it's a raffle prize. "You don't want to risk losing any of its magic."

My blood turns to ice. "I-I-don't know what you're talking about."

"Oh, I think you do. A reliable source"—Hunter's eyes flick to Duncan again—"told me that you think your bobblehead's granting you wishes."

"No I don't." My voice cracks. I try to cover it with a cough.

Hunter twists the bobblehead's neck until it's about to snap. "Then you won't mind if I do this?"

I shrug. "It's just my silly sister playing tricks on me."

With a flick of Hunter's wrist, Carey Price's head pops off. Hunter stands there with the body in one hand and the head in the other, the spring dangling between them, waiting for me to respond.

I don't. I can't. My body's as stiff as the Stanley Cup. If I open my mouth, I have no control over what might come out.

"My sisters are like that too," says Gray.

Tension broken—in the room, not in me—Hunter hands me the head. I toss it at the garbage can.

"Swish," says Jerry-Horn.

Hunter throws the body in after it. "And slam dunk."

Swallowing back tears—and a whole lot of pride—I tug off the rest of my gear as fast as I can. For the first time ever, I'm the first out of the dressing room.

I don't look back.

"Are you sure you want to leave the bobblehead in the garbage?" Duncan asks as we get into Coach Matt's car. "I can run back and get it for you."

I don't respond. Aislyn might have put the bobblehead in my bag. But it was obvious from the way Hunter talked that Duncan's the one who told him about the magic.

Maybe he's trying to make up for ratting me out. But unless he apologizes, I'm never talking to him again.

He calls my house on Sunday night, but I refuse to come to the phone. On Monday I walk to school without him. I don't sit next to him at lunch. Or go over to his house after school.

Like all best friends, we've had arguments before. Usually over something little, like whether a puck went over the goal line in mini sticks. Nothing that can't be sorted out by a good wrestling match.

This is different. I was trying so hard to fit in—to really be part of the team. Why did Duncan have to tell everyone the one secret that could turn me into more of an outcast than before?

There's nothing worse than not being able to trust your best friend. But, as much as I never want to speak to him ever again, it obvious at practice on Wednesday that I have to patch things up. No one mentions the bobblehead, but avoiding Duncan really makes it look like I have something to hide.

Besides, I miss him. And he must have a good reason for telling Hunter about the bobblehead.

I can't imagine what that good reason could be. But I really hope there is one.

When the bell rings on Thursday, I go to Duncan's locker. Duncan raises his eyebrows in surprise but says nothing. Like we've done a thousand times before—just not this week—we walk out of the school. Together.

It's a sunny December afternoon. The distant mountains are covered in snow, but the pavement in town is clear. Even though it's cold, I know Duncan's cousins will be waiting to play street hockey when we get to his house.

I'm right.

Duncan and I get picked for opposite teams. I volunteer to go in net—of course. Whenever Duncan gets a chance, he shoots at me like he's aiming to kill. Most of his shots go in, even though I'm trying as hard as I can.

"CAR!"

Two players from my team come over and help me drag the net to the side of the street. They do the same thing on the other side. We've got the routine mastered. But this time when the car's gone, no one moves the nets back into the middle of the road.

One of Duncan's cousin blows on his hands. "I can't feel my fingers. I'm done."

We carry all the stuff up Duncan's driveway and into the garage. Everyone scatters, leaving Duncan and me alone. The silence is even more awkward now than it was on the way home, so I ask him if he wants to keep playing. We've played in the garage before, usually when there's too much slush on the street and we're making too much noise in the basement for Coach Matt to watch TV. "I can put the goalie gear back on."

Duncan says no.

"How about we get slushies at the gas station?" I suggest.

"It's too cold. Plus I've got to do my homework."

I don't get why Duncan's being like this. *I'm* supposed to be the one who's mad at *him*. "It's only four o'clock!"

"Dad will be home any minute." Duncan looks down the street like he's actually hoping to see his dad's car. "We're eating early so we can get to the rink."

"Why? We don't have a practice, do we?"

"No." Duncan closes the garage, forcing us both onto the driveway. "It's just me and Hunter. His dad wants to put him through some shooting drills. We booked the kids' rink."

1, super shooter, 2, great goalie, 3, not me—

"Why are you still hanging out with that jerk?" The words erupt out, burning my throat.

"His dad—"

"Whatever," I snap. "Must be nice to have hockey parents."

"Give me a break," Duncan snaps back. "Having parents that are into hockey isn't the dream come true you imagine it to be. Your parents let you play. That's enough. You've got all the support you need. And I'm sick of you feeling sorry for yourself."

Without another word, Duncan goes into his house and slams the door behind him.

CHAPTER 31

Even though the bobblehead's sitting in a dumpster at the back of the arena where all the snow piles up, I get a shutout in both games on the weekend—an away game against the Eagles on Saturday and a home game against the Hitmen super early on Sunday morning. The Blazers don't get many goals. It's hard to believe we're the same team that scored so easily against the Eagles just a month ago.

I'm pretty sure Aislyn's the one who put the bobblehead in my hockey bag, but she's been so busy with her project that I haven't bothered to ask her. Or maybe it's because I'm afraid to find out she didn't do it. Then I'll have no logical explanation at all.

There are too many things happening that have no logical explanation. But this is the one that gets to me most: *How can the bobblehead still be working its magic when it's as good as dead?*

On Sunday afternoon Mom drags me out on the campaign trail. The election's tomorrow, and she needs all the help she can get.

We go door to door. If no one's home, we leave a flyer. If someone is home, we talk to them. Mom's not really trying to convince undecided voters to vote for her. She thinks it's too late for that. Instead she's making sure everyone has a way to get to the polls so they can cast a ballot.

Even though we're not begging for votes, I feel nervous every time someone comes to the door. I don't want another experience like the one with the guy who didn't want bees in the city or a sign on his lawn. Or worse—a run-in with another Mrs. Escobar.

Just as the tips of my fingers are starting to freeze, we get to a newly built house in a neighborhood across the bridge. It has Christmas lights strung up, and there's a wooden snowman with a crooked smile standing next to the door. I cross my fingers that the people inside are as nice as their decorations.

Mom rings the doorbell. I hear a dog barking inside. I rock back and forth on my heels as we wait for someone to answer. I stare down at the rainbow heart on their welcome mat. A light appears in the window next to the door. There are heavy footsteps, followed by the sound of dog claws skittering on hardwood floors.

The door opens. I take a step back. I know the man standing there, of course, but it's shocking to see him outside the arena, in his everyday clothes.

"Jelly!" Coach Tibor exclaims. "What are you doing here?"

Mom raises her eyebrows. It's probably the first time she's heard my nickname. I want to tell her it's a good thing, but I'm not sure it is anymore. Just like I'm not sure of anything.

I introduce Mom, who explains why we're standing on his front doorstep.

"Come on in!" Coach Tibor picks up the small black dog jumping at his leg and opens the door wider. "You can meet my partner, Doug, and warm up a bit."

I've seen Doug at the arena a few times, but I've never talked to him. He is taller and wider than Coach Tibor, with a warm smile.

"Hi, Elliot," he says, holding out his hand to shake. "I sure enjoy watching your team play."

"Thanks." I want to ask if he plays hockey too, but he's already turned his attention to Mom.

"You must be so proud of your son," he says to her. "Tibor can't believe how well he's doing in goal."

"Oh yes," she says. "Very proud."

All season I've wanted to make Mom proud. But hearing her say it doesn't fill me with joy like it's supposed to. Instead that feeling of being a fraud comes creeping back.

I stare into the house, wishing I could somehow disappear inside it. From the front entrance I can see one end of the kitchen and how it opens up into a large sitting area with a view of the river. It looks warm and inviting.

While Mom talks about election stuff with Doug, Coach Tibor asks me how I'm enjoying the Blazers. It's basically the same question Coach Matt asked. But he's asking it in a different way. Like he doesn't already know the answer.

I pet the dog, then say, "Good, I guess."

"That's not very convincing," he says. "Playing in net can be a lot of pressure."

I stare at the floor so Coach Tibor can't see the wetness forming in the corner of my eyes. No one's talked much about pressure, but that's exactly what I feel. Pressure to win. Pressure to fit in. Pressure to keep secrets.

"I'm worried about what's going to happen when Hunter's ready to play," I finally say. "I guess everyone will be relieved to have him back in net."

"I wouldn't say that," Coach Tibor replies. "Besides, there's room on the team for two goalies, you know."

I pick at the skin around my thumbnail. "I know," I say, even though I'm not sure I do. "It's just that everyone prefers Hunter." And then for some reason I add, "Especially Duncan."

"I thought you and Duncan were best friends."

"We were. I mean, we are." I can't believe I just said *were*. This is Duncan we're talking about, the best friend I've ever had. Until…

Before I know it, I'm telling Coach Tibor how Duncan betrayed me. I leave out the part about the secret involving a magic bobblehead, though. Coach Tibor's the one who taught me how to play in net. I don't want him to know that my skill in goal has more to do with magic than coaching.

"I don't remember much about being your age," Coach Tibor says. "But I do know this: good friends are hard to come by. You should talk to him. Ask him why he did it."

I wasn't looking for advice on how to patch things up with Duncan. But it suddenly seems clear that I have to fix at least one of the messed-up things in my life.

I didn't ask Duncan why he told Hunter about the magic because I was too scared of the answer. But I know I can't hide from the truth forever.

"Thanks, Coach Tibor. That's exactly what I'm going to do."

When Mom runs out of flyers, we head home. The sky's getting dark, and the Christmas lights come to life. Even the lights on the bridge seem festive.

Or maybe I'm just relieved about surviving the last of the campaign stuff. One more day until Mom is elected mayor. One more day until things go back to normal.

I plan to call Duncan as soon as we get home. But the instant we walk in the door, Dad tells Mom to call Grandma. Then he asks—no, he *tells* Aislyn and me to help him in the kitchen.

Mom goes all the way up to her bedroom to make the call, which is strange. Also strange is how distracted Dad is as he gives us dinner-making instructions.

Mom's not on the phone very long. When she comes back into the kitchen, her eyes glisten under the fluorescent lights.

Dad hands her a tissue. "Family meeting?"

Without waiting for her to answer, he turns off the water boiling on the stove and puts the pasta sauce on simmer. The onion-and-garlic smell hanging over the kitchen suddenly seems bitter compared to the warm and cozy scent of Coach

Tibor's house. I wish we'd stayed for tea like he and Doug wanted us to.

But I'm done with wishes. And I can tell by the look on Mom's face that onion and garlic are the least of my worries.

Her voice cracks as she says, "Grandpa has cancer."

CHAPTER 32

Grandpa needs surgery to have a tumor removed. It's booked for December 20—the last day of school. Mom and Dad say we have to carry on as usual and have faith that Grandpa will be okay. "As usual" seems like something that will never be possible again, just like my idea that everything could go "back to normal."

When dinner's done I head straight to my room. Just walking up the stairs makes me as tired as an out-of-shape hockey player at training camp. Shoving a pile of dirty clothes to the side, I drop into bed.

A soft knock startles me awake. I sit up and wipe the sleep from my eyes. "Come in?"

It's Aislyn. "What are you doing?"

"Hitchhiking to Hong Kong. What does it look like I'm doing?"

I have no idea why I said this. I don't like it any more now than I did when Hunter said it at the Smokies game. It's like Hunter's always on my mind these days.

Aislyn rolls her eyes. "That doesn't even make sense."

"Whatever." I pull my weighted blanket around me. Mom bought it to help me calm down—it's *scientifically proven to reduce stress and anxiety*. "What are *you* doing?"

"Mom and Dad made me come up to see if you need help with your math homework."

How could anyone think about math at a time like this? "Thanks, but I'd rather brush my teeth with *your* toothbrush."

Aislyn ignores the dig. "Mom thought it would be a good distraction."

"From what? The possibility that Grandpa might die?"

Tears spring to her eyes. "I'm upset about Grandpa too."

Someone should seal my mouth with duct tape. "I know. I'm sorry."

Aislyn wipes her cheeks with the sleeve of her shirt. "I also wanted to give you this." From behind her back she pulls out a bobblehead.

I stand up to make sure I'm seeing right. I am. It's Carey Price. "You bought me a new one?"

"No, I rescued the old one."

"From the trash?"

"Duncan brought it to me. Then we put the head back on together. Good as new. See?" She shoves it into my hands.

I jostle it a little—as if I'm afraid it might bite me or something. Carey Price's head bobbles at me like a long-lost friend. "But why?"

"I'm the one who put it in your hockey bag."

Even though I had assumed it was Aislyn, I'm relieved to hear her say it. If it wasn't her, there was no other explanation—

besides something that could only be described as next-level magic.

"I didn't do it to cause you trouble," she continues. "I did it because—"

"You really believe it's magic?" I can't keep the hope out of my voice.

"Not really," she replies kindly. "But you do. And that's all that matters."

For some reason, her kindness irritates me. I raise my voice. "You're the one who said there was some type of genie hiding in there! Go on, summon your own master! Make a wish for Grandpa. Make a wish to finally complete your project. Make a wish for—"

She blinks three times, really fast. For a second I'm worried she's going to start crying all over again. Instead she asks, "You know how in *Aladdin* Jaffar always wanted more power? And Aladdin wanted more help even though he promised to free the genie? That's how it works. No matter how many wishes you have, you always want more."

I stare down at the bobblehead that's somehow made it back into my hands. Aislyn's right. I *do* want more wishes. I don't want to be a goalie who never lets in a single goal. I don't want to be a hockey player who yells at his teammates and hits his opponents. I don't want to be a terrible friend to Duncan or a bad brother to Aislyn. And I don't want to be a son who breaks his promises. But, more than anything, I *do* want to be a good grandson.

I'd do anything to have a wish left for Grandpa.

Aladdin almost died because he wanted to be—or *appear* to be—something he wasn't. Because he thought he deserved more. And when he lost the magic lamp, didn't he come close to destroying the entire kingdom?

I look up. Aislyn's gone.

My grip tightens around Carey Price. The bedroom's suddenly too hot for me to breathe. I rush to the window and pull it open.

Without a second thought, I hurl the bobblehead out the window. It flies above the small fence separating our house from the neighbor's. I'm sure I see Carey Price grin as he sails toward their roof.

It hits the shingles first. Then the entire doll—head, stick, body, skates—breaks into a million pieces. As plastic bits roll down the roof and onto the grass below, something inside me breaks too.

CHAPTER 33

Election day. It's hard to concentrate in class. If it's not Grandpa I'm thinking about, it's Duncan.

I really need to talk to him. To find out why he did it. He pulled my bobblehead out of the garbage, after all. And not just any garbage—a locker-room garbage full of apple cores and Band-Aids and other disgusting stuff I don't even want to think about. Was it because he felt guilty?

But Duncan's still avoiding me, so I never get the chance to ask.

At the end of the day an announcement comes over the PA. "Would Elliot and Aislyn Feldner-Martel please come to the office?"

At first I think Mom might have news about the election. This isn't one of those big-city events where candidates gather at election headquarters with staff and supporters, prepared to give an acceptance or concession speech. In Trail, candidates just go about their business, waiting for city staff to count the ballots and call out results.

Then I realize it could also be news about Grandpa. Mom said nothing was expected to change before the surgery. But how could she be so sure? I overheard Mom and Dad talking late into the night about how much information Grandma and Grandpa had kept from her.

It's not Mom waiting for us at the office. It's Dad. "I thought I'd drive you home since I was here anyway," he says.

I want to know why he was at the school, but before I get a chance, Aislyn asks whether there are any updates on the election.

"We won't know anything until tonight."

It's clear from the tilt of Dad's chin that he doesn't want us to ask any more questions. Twirling a piece of hair around her finger, Aislyn keeps quiet for the entire ride. I stare out the window and nibble my nails down to nubs.

When we get home, Mom's sitting at the kitchen table with a cup of tea. She gives us a small smile.

"Family meeting," Dad announces.

Oh no. Two family meetings in two days. Not good.

As if to prove me right, Mom tells Aislyn to go up to her room.

Warning bells go off in my head. "How can we have a family meeting without Aislyn?"

"I shouldn't have called it a family meeting," Dad says. "This is about you, E."

The warning bell turns into a foghorn. *Danger ahead.*

Once Aislyn's gone, Dad pulls a piece of paper out of the clipboard he always carries. This is not a sketch for one of his carvings, though. It's the math test—with Dad's forged signature at the bottom.

My heart drops so fast it's like a hole's opened up in the earth's crust.

They start firing questions at me—all variations on the same two things. Why did I fake Dad's signature, and why haven't I been doing my schoolwork like I promised I would?

"What's the point?" I fire back. "No matter how hard I try, I'll never be as good as Aislyn!"

"We don't want you to be as good as Aislyn," Mom says. "We just want you to be as good as you can be."

"You say that, but Aislyn's the one who gets all the attention." Emotion swirls inside me, making my head spin faster than a goal light. "She's the one who does everything right."

"That's not true, E," says Dad.

"Then why do you take her to all her robotics stuff and never take me to hockey?" The words come flying out of my mouth so fast that I have no control over them. "You haven't been to one single game!"

"Oh." Dad seems startled. For once, he's at a loss for words.

I chew my pinkie nail—the only one that's still got some length to it—and wait for someone to say something. Anything.

"I'm not sure why I didn't realize that was important to you," he finally says. "I guess I figured you were happy going with Mr. Bilenki, someone who actually knows something about hockey."

"Besides, your dad's been really busy since I entered the mayoral—"

"That's no excuse, Esme." Dad folds his hands on the table. "There's always time for something important. And I know how important hockey is to you, E. I'm sorry."

This is not what I expected to happen at the beginning of the family meeting. It feels great to be heard. And I'm not as uncomfortable as I was that time in the car during our last heart-to-heart. If only I'd told him earlier how much I wanted him to see me play, instead of waiting for it to come out now.

"I understand, Dad. I mean, you have been busy. And you know that talk we had in the car?" I wait for him to nod before continuing, "I want you to know that you support this family just fine. We have everything we need." I got this from Duncan, but since he said it, I've realized it's true. And it doesn't just apply to hockey.

"Thanks, E." He reaches out and touches my arm. "And again—I'm sorry."

My mouth has gone dry, and my throat feels tight. Somehow I manage to say, "It's okay." And I mean it.

Dad wipes a fist across the corner of his eye before getting up to give me a hug. "We still have to talk about your school-work, though."

Mom's phone beeps, and she glances at it. She must be waiting for election results. Why did I always have to make things harder for her by messing everything up?

"You have practice in thirty minutes," she says.

"But you're not going," adds Dad.

My parents exchange one of those looks that says a thousand things at once. Mom nods. "No more hockey until you've finished all the assignments you've missed. In every subject."

It hits me like I've been bodychecked into the boards. I worked so hard to be part of the Blazers. If only I'd found time to work that hard on school as well. Like Dad said, there's always time for things that are important. I screwed up. And now I am about to lose my spot on the team.

The spot I worked so hard to get.

CHAPTER 34

Before we even get up from the table, I've made up my mind. I will catch up on my schoolwork, make things right with Duncan and get back on the Blazers as soon as possible.

"Can I call Duncan?" I ask as Dad starts pulling vegetables out of the fridge for dinner.

Dad tells me to make it quick.

Which is not hard. Because Duncan doesn't answer.

Is he at the rink? With Hunter?

I don't have time to think about it before the phone in my hand rings. "Hello?"

"Why do you want to talk to me?" asks Duncan.

"Why *don't* you want to talk to me?" It's not the way I intended to start the conversation. But the speech I had all prepared when I called him has vanished from my mind.

"You're the one who chilled me out. After the...bobble-head-in-the-dressing-room scene."

"Yeah!" I respond louder than I meant to. "Because I was mad at you for doing it."

"Doing what?" he asks.

"Telling Hunter about the bobblehead."

"I didn't tell Hunter anything." Duncan's voice is flat.

I pause. "Then how did he know it was magic?"

"Your sister."

Wait. What?

"Aislyn told me you guys rescued the doll," I say slowly, trying to think things through as I go. "And that she's the one who put it in my hockey bag. But she never talked to Hunter."

"She didn't have to," Duncan says. "Hunter was just repeating some of the stuff she wrote in the note."

The notepaper taped to the bobblehead. I should've known that Aislyn wouldn't make any kind of gesture without writing an essay of explanation to go along with it.

"You thought it was me?" asks Duncan.

I'm so glad Duncan can't see my face right now. I've been the worst friend ever. "Uh…"

"Whatever. I've got to go."

"No, wait!" This is where I should apologize. Instead I start talking fast. "I got rid of the bobblehead for good. So I'm going back to being the terrible player I was last season and—"

"How do you know you're going to be terrible? It's time to start believing in yourself instead of some plastic doll."

I'm about to tell him it's not a doll—not that it matters—when there's a knock on my bedroom door. "Can I call you back?" I ask, my voice shaking.

"Don't call me. I'll call you. Maybe. When I have time to talk." There's a loud click on the other end of the line as Duncan hangs up on me.

I put down the phone and open the door, expecting Aislyn. But I'm wrong. Again.

It's Mom. "I lost the election," she says.

As she takes a seat next to me on the bed, I try to figure out what to say. I thought for sure she'd win. After all that hard work, how could she not?

Mom sniffs. "I'm okay, Elliot."

"Really? Because if it were me, I would so *not* be okay."

"I was the dark horse. I knew that when I entered the election. It's the golden rule of politics—you have to be willing to lose."

The more I learn about politics, the more it reminds me of sports. And not in a good way.

"Still, I didn't expect to be this disappointed." Mom takes a deep breath. "But it's for the best. This election put a lot of pressure on all of us. I don't think you'd be struggling if I'd been around more. And being mayor would've been even more of a challenge. This way I can watch you play. Hopefully, come to your tournament in Penticton."

Knowing Mom believes I'll get back on the ice this season makes me feel a tiny bit better. But even if I'd realized that things would *not* go back to normal if Mom was elected—even if I'd realized losing would mean she'd actually watch me play—I still would've wanted her to win. I think I might be more disappointed than Mom is. "Why did you do all that if you didn't expect to win?"

"Lots of reasons. It was good experience. Good for business. And if I run again in four years, I know I'll do a lot better."

Four years seems like a very long time. Still, I'm glad she's willing to try again.

"I bet it would be easier if politics ran in the family or something," I say.

"What do you mean, honey?"

"Like the Gretzky family or the Subban family. You know—being born in a hockey family has big advantages. If you want to play hockey, that is."

Mom smiles. "True. That might make things easier," she says. "But the best achievements are the ones you earn on your own."

CHAPTER 35

Without hockey, I have lots of time to do schoolwork.

Instead of feeling sorry for myself, I try to remember that everyone has their struggles. I reread the book about Carey Price. I had forgotten that he left home when he was fifteen to live with another family, in Pasco, Washington, so he could play for an amateur league. He had to deal with injuries and didn't get the same opportunities as other players just because he was Indigenous.

We learned about residential schools at school. I shared what I had learned about Fred Sasakamoose from the book I'd read with Mom. Fred said it was more of a work colony than a school. Residential schools weren't mentioned in the Carey Price book but, like my teacher said, that doesn't mean they didn't have an impact on Carey Price and his family. Along with all the other bad things that happened to Indigenous people because of colonization.

Despite all that history, Carey Price has won both the Hart Memorial and the Vezina Trophy, and he almost won the Stanley Cup. Plus, he's one of the highest-paid goalies ever. And he uses his money for good stuff, like donating hockey gear to the minor hockey league he played for in Williams Lake and funding a breakfast program in his hometown of Anahim Lake.

Thinking about what I learned in those books often made me think about Grandpa. Worrying about him and his surgery breaks my concentration on schoolwork every time I think about it. Which is often.

I wish there was something I could do. I've sent him emails, but I haven't been allowed to talk to him. Not being able to help is pretty much the worst feeling ever—and I've had a lot of experience with bad feelings over these past few months— but it's nothing compared to battling cancer.

At school I study in the library instead of having lunch at the hockey table because I don't want to face my teammates. No one seems to notice. Or care. Until one day when Jerry-Horn pulls me aside between classes.

"Where've you been, Jelly?"

I lean back against a row of lockers. "Around."

"Word on the street is that you're grounded."

"That pretty much sums it up." I shrug like it's no big deal.

"Let me know if you need help, Jelly. I'm ace in English, and I have some buddies who are good at math. Anything to get you back on the ice. We miss you."

I wish he didn't know the details of my trouble in school. If Jerry-Horn knows, everyone knows. But I'm tired of keeping secrets. And besides, it's the last thing he said that makes my throat feel tight.

They've got Hunter back in net. I know because Mom ran into Mrs. Escobar at the store. He's not getting shutouts, but he's doing really well. I was happy when I heard that the Blazers are still winning most of their games. And also kind of sad, because it means they really don't need me anymore.

"You miss me?"

"Of course." Jerry-Horn nudges my shoulder. It's barely more than a tap, but it pretty much knocks me over. "You're part of the team, aren't you?"

The bell rings in time with the fireworks going off inside me.

Cheesy, I know. But not an exaggeration. There aren't enough fireworks in the world to describe how good it feels to be missed.

We have a field trip to the museum on the last day of school, so I don't get another chance to have lunch with my team before the end of the year. When the bus drops us off, I go straight home, hoping there'll be an update on Grandpa.

There's not.

No one's around except for Aislyn, who's in her room working on her project. Too distracted to even play video games, I scroll through hockey videos on YouTube while I wait…and wait…and wait.

An hour later Mom and Dad finally come home. Together.

"Aislyn, can you come down here?" Dad calls up the stairs.

Mom enters the den. Her facial expression's impossible to read. "Do you have an update on Grandpa?" I ask her.

She leans down and kisses my forehead. "Wait for your sister."

Normally I'd wipe the kiss away. Today I don't.

Aislyn bursts into the den, her face flushed. "What happened?"

"Grandpa's all right," Mom says. "He made it through surgery, but they're keeping him overnight for observation."

A shiver runs down my spine. "What does that mean? I thought it was day surgery."

"They're just being cautious. He's old and so is Grandma, and there's no other family around to help out."

"So he's okay now?" It almost seems too good to be true. "We can stop worrying?"

"They'll have to study the tumor, right?" asks Aislyn.

"Pathology testing will tell us whether he needs more treatment," Mom replies. "But we won't get the results until the new year. Until then we shouldn't worry. Worrying never makes things better. It just makes them bigger."

"Did you talk to him?" I ask.

"No, I talked to Grandma."

"Will we ever get to talk to him?" Even though I'm a bit scared about what I might see, I want Grandpa's face to appear on the laptop screen. I want him to reassure me that everything's going to be okay.

"Eventually…" Mom puts her hand on my knee. "For now Grandpa's using all his energy to get better. In the meantime, he would want you both to keep doing your thing."

My thing, of course, is hockey. And after this, I'm more determined than ever before.

CHAPTER 36

Every day during winter break I do three things:

1. Catch up on schoolwork (while chewing lots of spearmint gum).
2. Suffer through a list of dryland training exercises (which keeps getting longer).
3. Shovel driveways and sidewalks (whenever there's snow).
4. Think about talking to Duncan.

Here's what I don't do:

1. Talk to Duncan.
2. Talk to Duncan.
3. Talk to Duncan.

On the first day back at school, I hand in everything and write three makeup tests. I don't ace any of them, but I don't think I'll come close to failing either. Everything makes a lot more sense now that I've done the assignments.

I'm starving when the bell finally rings to end the day—probably because I studied over lunch and barely managed to finish the turkey soup Dad thawed for me.

I'm also determined. If I can get through all that homework, I can make things right with Duncan. I know I can.

I rush to his locker so he can't leave without me. "Hey, Duncan! Wait up!"

"What do you want?" he asks, slamming his locker door shut.

"Can I walk home with you?"

Duncan shrugs but doesn't say no. We walk out of the school, letting the sound of the busy hallways fill the silence between us. Litter covers the floors, which still reek of bleach from the extra scrubbing they got over the holidays.

"I'm sorry," I say when we're finally out in the fresh, crisp air of the schoolyard.

"For what?"

I feel like I'm standing in the middle of a frozen pond, on melting ice that's already too thin. "I'm sorry for thinking you told Hunter," I say. "You know, about the bobblehead."

Duncan shoves his hands deeper into his pockets as we turn down his block. "We're best friends, Elliot. I would never do that to you."

"I know. It was all the magic stuff, I guess. I just stopped thinking straight." I'm not proud of what I have to say next, but I know I have to say it. "Things weren't going well for me, and you were hanging out with Hunter. It made me jealous."

Duncan's shoulders relax a bit. "I know you're worried about Hunter. But he's worried about you too, you know."

"Hunter? Worried about me?"

"You were a rookie getting all these shutouts," Duncan says. "And he's always had to work so hard."

I kick a loose piece of ice down the sidewalk. When we catch up to it, Duncan gives it a kick.

We continue like that, taking turns, just like we used to do with rocks when we were kids.

"Is that why he's so mean?" I give the ice chunk an extra-hard kick. It breaks apart, scattering everywhere but going nowhere.

"Dad says he doesn't know any better. He's just treating us the way his dad treats him."

I think about this for a minute. "That doesn't make it okay, though. Especially when he talks rudely about girls."

"You're right about that. But I think he feels threatened by them just like he feels threatened by you. When it comes to hockey, he probably feels threatened by everyone." Duncan lowers his voice, even though there's no one around to overhear. "Hunter told me that he hates hockey sometimes. Because of the pressure his dad puts on him."

Turkey soup rises in my throat. How could anyone as good as Hunter hate hockey?

"That's harsh." Remembering that day in the school parking lot—when Hunter's dad was so awful to him (even though he'd done nothing wrong) and my dad was so not-awful to me (even though I had)—I feel sorry for Hunter all over again.

Not everyone in my family loves hockey. But they do love me.

"Want to play mini sticks?" Duncan asks as we turn the corner onto his street.

"You bet I do."

And for the first time in a long time, playing hockey's fun again.

When I get home, I do my exercises and finish my homework—all before dinner. It feels great to be back on schedule.

Mom and Dad are back on schedule too. Mom comes home after the store closes at five. Dad comes up from the studio shortly after that and starts banging around in the kitchen.

But when we're called to the table, I can tell something's not quite right. "Mom?"

"Is it Grandpa?" asks Aislyn.

Mom's mouth twitches. "We'll talk about it after dinner."

Dad dishes out ratatouille casserole from a big dish in the middle of the table. "You should tell them now."

"Grandpa got his results back." Mom's voice shakes. "They didn't get all the cancer. He needs more treatment."

"Is he going to be okay?" I know it's not a simple question. But I want a simple answer.

"He's got good doctors," Dad says. "But Grandma needs help looking after him at home. So Mom's going to stay with them for a while."

The kitchen's so silent, the humming of the fridge sounds louder than the New York Rangers' goal horn. "When are you going?"

Mom takes a deep breath. "Wednesday."

"You'll miss the Change Climate Change contest!"

I can't believe Aislyn's thinking about that contest. Then again, I kind of can, because the first thing I thought of was hockey.

"I'm sorry," Mom says. "And I'll miss Elliot's tournament this weekend too. I had a hotel room booked for all of us."

"It's okay, Mom. We'll be okay. This is more important," I say. And as much as I want Mom to come to my tournament, I mean it. "I can go with Duncan and Coach Matt."

"They're staying with Mr. Bilenki's cousin," Dad says. "I'm going to take you. But only if you've caught up on all your schoolwork."

Before I can respond, Aislyn slumps back in her seat and crosses her arms over her chest. "What about me?"

"You'll come with us to Penticton."

"I have to spend all weekend watching hockey?"

"Yes." Dad folds his hands on the table. "And Elliot's coming to support you at your contest."

I wanted Dad to come watch me play. Now I am getting so much more than that. He is coming to watch a whole tournament. And, as a bonus, my sister is coming too.

There's just one problem. I have no idea what they're going to see.

Will I be riding the bench? Getting scored on in net? Or skating out as forward on my jelly legs?

The only thing I know for sure is, if I don't get my schoolwork done, there will be nothing to see at all.

CHAPTER 37

The next day I double-check that I've handed in all my school-work. I've done everything. But according to the deal I made with Mom and Dad, it all has to be marked before I can get back on the ice.

I really want to join my team for practice that night. I know it's a long shot, but I cross and uncross my fingers all day, hoping Mr. Morrisette and Ms. Deadmarsh have performed a miracle and finished all the marking in one night.

They haven't.

Wednesday comes and goes—still nothing.

By Thursday I'm as desperate as a free agent in a scoring drought. If I don't get everything back today, I can't play tomorrow.

Duncan says the coaches have decided Hunter and I will take turns in net during the tournament. If I'm there. If not, it will be all Hunter.

At least I know I won't be playing out. Still, the idea of Hunter taking my place for the whole tournament—and maybe for the whole season, since I'm starting to think my schoolwork will never get marked—makes me feel sick. Knowing that it's all my fault for handing in so much late work makes me feel even worse.

I walk into Mr. Morrisette's classroom after lunch on Thursday like I'm wearing skates—without guards—on a hardwood floor. As soon as he sees me, Mr. Morrisette pulls a pile of papers out of his messenger bag and waves it like a white flag. "You don't even have to ask. I have it right here."

I melt into a puddle of relief. He tells me I did well on the assignments and tests. There's just a few small things he'd like to go over with me. I'm listening. But I'm not. All I can think about is that I'm halfway there. If Ms. Deadmarsh comes through, I can play tomorrow.

All hope disappears when I walk into English. A substitute teacher hovers over Ms. Deadmarsh's desk. She looks like she's had a tough day, and I doubt she knows anything about my unmarked schoolwork.

I collapse into my seat and spend the rest of the period picturing Hunter hogging the net all weekend. In the same split-screen image, I'm on the couch playing video games. Alone. Again.

The bell rings. Everyone slams their books shut and gathers up their things. "Uh, which one of you is Elliot?" the sub calls out over the noise.

Duncan and I exchange glances. I don't dare get my hopes up, but I didn't do anything to get in trouble so maybe... just maybe...

I fight my way through the crowd of kids funneling out of the classroom. Tomorrow's a professional development day. Even though it's the start of a long weekend, no one's in a hurry to get out of the school. In the aisles between desks, my class-mates stand around making plans and chatting with their friends like they may never see them again.

Somehow I finally make it to the front of the room. "I'm Elliot."

She hands me a paper bag full of papers. "Ms. Deadmarsh left this for you."

"I'll get Dad to pick you up for practice," Duncan says when we get to my locker. "It's awesome to have you back."

I'm sure Duncan's exaggerating with the *awesome* bit. Since we made up, he's been extra careful about doing—or not doing—anything to make me feel jealous over Hunter. I like to think he doesn't need to. Still, I'm happy to hear the Blazers want me back.

Not happy about what I have to say next, though.

"Bad news about practice." I grab my stuff and close the door. "I can't make it tonight. I have to go to this thing for Aislyn."

It's been a month since I've been on the ice with the Blazers. I should really get in at least one practice before the tournament. But there's no way. Dad's not one to break a rule, especially when he's the one who made it. Mom's gone to Quebec to be with Grandma and Grandpa, so I can't get her to change his mind.

"Is it that climate-change thing?"

I'm impressed that he remembered. I nod and start walking a bit faster. I need to get home to help Aislyn finish up her display.

Most of the work's done. She just has to attach everything to her poster board. I was surprised she asked for my help, even if it's just cutting and pasting.

I'm embarrassed to admit that I don't even know what project Aislyn ended up doing after giving up on the algae bioreactor, solar water heater and wearable wind turbine. Guess I'm about to find out.

It doesn't take me long to figure out that my sister's project is the best one in the gym.

Before Dad and I have even finished helping her set up, her plastic pulverization machine—made from a bunch of outdated lab equipment she collected from the local college— is surrounded by people interested in watching her demonstration. She puts a bunch of single-use plastic containers in a round cylinder that reminds me of a mini dryer, closes the lid and turns it on. There's lots of noise as the machine gets to work, shredding, then heating, then molding the plastic into something new.

"We really need to stop producing plastic from petroleum by-products," she tells the crowd. "But for now, this machine can reduce both plastic waste and fossil-fuel consumption because the discarded plastic doesn't have to be shipped around the world to be recycled. Wouldn't it be great if there was one on every kitchen counter in the world?"

Everyone claps when Aislyn finishes her speech. People look at her display—which includes photos of the machine as it was being built and a full description of how the system works—but everyone's much more interested in seeing empty yogurt containers and milk jugs transform into Lego blocks.

As the evening goes on, I realize I wasn't jealous of only Hunter. It was Aislyn too. Just like I wanted to be naturally good at hockey, I wanted to be naturally smart like my sister.

But watching her explain her invention to the judges, I also realize how hard she's worked. Being naturally good at something is just the beginning. It's what you do with it that counts.

Aislyn wins third place. She gets beat by an eleventh-grade team that created a prototype for an electric-powered bamboo car and by a tenth grader who didn't create anything at all but wrote out a strategy—with a thousand equations I didn't understand—for moving the earth away from the sun.

Instead of being disappointed, Aislyn sees it as a challenge. "I'm only in sixth grade. Imagine what I'll be doing by the time I'm their age."

"I do hope you'll keep trying." Dad smiles. "You know what they say—you miss 100 percent of the shots you don't take."

My mouth falls open in shock. "Did you just quote the Great One?"

"The great one of what?"

"You know, Wayne Gretzky? He's the one who said that."

"Oh, well, then I guess I did." Dad's smile grows wider. "Maybe there's even more to learn from hockey than I thought."

CHAPTER 38

We're just about to leave for Penticton on Friday morning when I get a video call from Grandpa.

"I got the good-luck charm you sent me." He holds a tiny piece of red-and-blue plastic up to the screen. If I squint, I can just make out the Canadiens logo.

I reach into my pocket and clutch the chunk of plastic I kept for myself. When I cleaned up the bobblehead mess in our yard and the neighbor's, I kept a few pieces for luck. I don't think I'll ever know whether the bobblehead was truly magic. But I figure it doesn't hurt to believe in something—as long as it doesn't stop me from believing in myself.

"It's just a silly superstition. But I want you to get better. And I didn't know how else to help."

"Thank you, Sport." He sounds like he swallowed a mouthful of gravel, but he doesn't look as green as he did the last time I saw him. "I'm going to keep it with me. That way you're here with me too. Nothing silly about it."

My throat closes up so tight, I can't even speak.

"Your mom tells me you've been having a rough time of it," Grandpa continues.

I'm not sure whether he's talking about my schoolwork or losing my temper or how I messed up with Duncan and the team. Not that it matters. Grandpa's the one who's sick. The last thing he should be worrying about is me. "I'm okay, Grandpa."

"Of course you are, Sport." Grandpa's smile is weak, and the cancer has taken some of the sparkle from his eyes. "I just want you to remember that there's nothing wrong with asking for help. I've always liked Carey Price, but you know what made me root for him even more?"

"What?"

"The time he entered the player assistance program to deal with his mental health."

Huh. I had forgotten about that. I guess Carey Price and I have even more in common than I thought.

Before I can respond Mom and Grandma appear on the screen next to Grandpa. "Your grandpa's been a total champ through all the chemo and radiation."

"Hi, Mom, hi, Gran." I fold and refold a napkin on the table to keep my hands busy. With all the stressful stuff that's been happening, I've got no nails left to chew. "So he's all done now?"

"The treatment's just started, Elliot." I see Mom glance at her parents. "Grandpa's still very sick."

"Cancer treatment's annoying like that." Aislyn turns the laptop so that both she and Dad are in the picture too. "It makes you sicker before it makes you better."

The napkin falls to the floor. Everyone else chats for a while. I stay quiet.

"Good luck in the tournament, Sport," Grandpa says when it's time for goodbye.

"Thanks." I can feel the plastic digging into my leg. "I'm going to need it."

I don't realize how nervous I am about being back in net until Dad drops me off at the arena. He and Aislyn are going to check in to the hotel, but Dad promises they'll be back for our first game of the tournament against the Vernon Vipers.

The Penticton Memorial Arena is old—older than any other place I've played, including the Civic Arena and the Pioneer Arena—which adds to my sense of dread. Walking down the dark hallway to the dressing room, I'm sure it must be haunted.

Coach Tibor meets me at the dressing-room door. "It's great to have you back, Elliot. I guess you know that Hunter's back too?"

I nod. "Duncan told me we're taking turns in net. Who's starting?"

The question ran through my mind the entire car ride here. I'm still not sure I want to know the answer, though. I'm scared to start after one month off. But the thought of watching Hunter be the star? That's equally terrifying.

"Hunter's dad wants him to rest, so you'll play the first game," Coach Tibor replies. I want to ask why Hunter needs to rest and what the plan is for the rest of the tournament. Before I can, Coach Tibor heads off. "I'll let you get ready."

When I open the dressing-room door, I'm greeted by a chorus of hellos and welcomes. Even Hunter—who's dressing for the game even though he's not playing—gives me a smile.

The attention feels good, but I'm relieved when everyone turns their attention back to getting ready. I need time—and a clear head—to go through my routine.

When I'm mostly dressed and munching on my granola bar, I start to feel calmer. No matter what happens out there, I'll be on the ice with my team. This isn't just about me anymore.

Right before we head out onto the ice, I put my piece of the bobblehead in the side pocket of my goalie pants. I think the pocket's supposed to be for extra padding. It has a new purpose now.

I feel okay during warm-up, but as I skate toward the net for the start of the game, my stomach flutters with nervous energy. I try a new thing Mom taught me for calming down.

Inhale with mouth closed and silently count to four, hold breath and silently count to five, exhale through mouth and silently count to six...repeat.

It works—sort of.

The ref blows the whistle and drops the puck. I crouch into position.

Madder wins the face-off, but the Vipers quickly gain possession. Their right-winger scoops up the puck and their entire line comes sailing across the blue line.

Right wing passes to center. Instead of stopping the puck and setting up for another pass, the Vipers player one-times a clapper of a shot.

The puck flies at me as if exploding from a rocket launcher.

Instead of going down, I stand my ground. The puck hits me right in the breadbasket, then bounces off my chest and drops to the ice. Only then do I fall to my knees to cover it.

"WAY TO GO, ELLIOT!" Aislyn's voice rings out over the cowbells. I glance over because I want to see my dad and my sister in the crowd with all the other Blazers families. But the stands aren't lit well, and the glass above the boards is so scratched, you can't see through it. Still, it's enough to know they're there.

By the end of the first period, being back in net feels comfortable—like putting on an old pair of sneakers. No one scores for either side. I have no idea whether there's magic involved, but I'm too focused on the game to give it much thought.

Five minutes into the second, Kali gets knocked over by a Viper who could be mistaken for a bulldozer. She lands hard but immediately scrambles to her feet and catches up to the play, totally unfazed.

The officials stop the game and clear the benches to clean the ice halfway through the second. It's above zero outside, and the rink manager's having trouble keeping the ice cold.

In the dressing room, I take off my gloves. "You're working hard, Jelly!" Coach Tibor nods toward my hands. They're steaming.

"Great job out there, Blazers," says Coach Matt. "Now listen up. We have to make a few changes. Kali's out."

"I think I bruised my butt." She laughs, so we do too. Still, we all know this is bad. After Madder, Kali's the toughest person on our team—only a real injury would keep her off the ice.

Coach Lisa switches Seven from forward to defense. Seven's good at skating backward, and he's been around hockey long enough to know all the positions.

Even so, it doesn't take long for us to fall into the hole Kali's left in the lineup. We're deep in the Vipers' zone when Seven creeps away from the blue line to gobble up a rebound. He winds up to shoot, but the puck gets nudged away at the last second.

Instantly the Vipers are on the breakaway. Three against none—unless you include me.

The player carrying the puck dekes to the left, then to the right, before sliding it over to the trailer, who's coming in fast on the short side.

I move sideways like they demonstrate on the *Great Goalie* YouTube channel, keeping my stick in front of me. The ice is smooth—too smooth—and I get tangled up, leaving an opening between my leg pads as I scramble to stay on my feet. The shot comes straight at me.

It's there. Then it's gone. Disappearing right through the five-hole.

The ref's whistle screams in my ear. "GOAL!"

CHAPTER 39

It's not the Vipers' last shot. And it's not their last goal. I play as hard as I can but still let in three more goals by the end of the second.

My teammates answer back in the third, but it's not enough. Final score, 4–6.

The game's not the only thing we lose. By the end of three, Fartsby (who pulled his groin trying to stay onside) and Jerry-Horn (who blocked a rocket shot with his pinkie finger) have joined Kali and Hunter on the bench.

To my surprise, no one's too disappointed by the loss. Including me. We still have fun in the dressing room afterward as Jerry-Horn blares another song from his playlist. I join a game of hot potato with Charlie's ball of sock tape, relieved that the bobblehead shutout streak is officially broken.

And I didn't completely suck in net without it.

There's no team dinner that night for three reasons:

1. We have an early game in the morning.
2. Some Blazers need medical attention (including

Hunter, who has to do an hour of exercises assigned by his physiotherapist and supervised by his dad).

3. All the restaurants are either booked up or don't want to serve hockey teams.

I'm super disappointed even when Dad tells me we're still going to go out for dinner with Gray and his family. The whole point of a tournament is being part of a group. Plus I'm worried about how my dad and sister will be accepted by a family like Gray's, who probably understand hockey in a way my dad never will. He may be able to quote Gretzky, but he still doesn't know the difference between offside in soccer—or football, as he calls it—and hockey.

But after Gray and I have gobbled up our greasy food, we play on the restaurant's foosball table while Aislyn colors with Gray's little sisters (who've attached themselves to her like limbs) and Dad talks to Gray's parents (who just happen to be British like him). It's almost as good as a full team event.

Plus it makes me realize something. Being myself and making friends is the very best part of fitting in.

I don't expect to start in net the next morning. I'm not looking forward to riding the pine—especially with Dad and Aislyn watching—but I know I'll get a chance to play again later this afternoon.

What I really don't expect is the bad news that floods our dressing room as the other Blazers trickle in. Kali's tailbone is actually fractured, Fartsby's groin injury is bad enough that he can't skate, and Jerry-Horn's hand is so swollen that he can't hold his stick.

Hunter plays well, but the game's a disaster. We go down, 3–7.

During our second match of the day, Seven leaves with a stomachache. "I hope it's not the flu," says Charlie. "Or some other new pandemic."

Kali smacks him across the chest. "It's too early to joke about the coronavirus."

"I'm not joking." Charlie pulls his jersey back in place. "COVID-19 wasn't the first pandemic to cancel the NHL. There were no playoffs in 1918 because of the Spanish flu."

It's not exactly comforting. But even with me in goal and one of our lead scorers throwing up in the bathroom, we somehow manage to scrape together a 5–5 tie.

There are eight teams in the tournament. Even though we've lost twice, the tie puts us into sixth place, with a shot at the finals. To get there, we need to beat the team that finished first in the round-robin.

"Another early game tomorrow," Coach Lisa announces during the pizza dinner Mrs. Escobar organized for the team in the hotel conference room Saturday night. "Dyne and Seven are both maybes."

"What happened to Dyne?" asks Fartsby.

"His stomach's upset too. He ate at the same place as Seven last night, so it might be food poisoning."

I stop chewing my pizza and accidentally swallow a big piece of hot cheese. It burns as it slides down my throat.

"So we're really going to have to juggle lines," Coach Lisa continues.

Duncan and I exchange a look that says something like *AHHHH!* Well, actually Duncan looks calm—like always—but I feel like I'm falling off a cliff.

It's my turn to play goal tomorrow. I've got *some* luck—I touch my pocket to make sure the plastic's still there—but the magic, if it was ever there, is definitely gone. How are we going to pull out a win with so many players on the bench?

Coach Matt offers a few inspirational words that do nothing to calm my nerves and tells us to try to get a good night's sleep.

"One more thing," adds Coach Tibor. "Because we're so short on players, we can't afford to dress two goalies. Elliot, you're playing out."

Coach Lisa puts me on a line with Madder and Charlie. My heart pounds against the chest protector I borrowed from Gray as we're sent out for our first shift. I take a deep breath—feeling very light without all my goalie equipment—and step off the bench. After three strong strides, I catch an edge and go sprawling across the ice.

I fall three more times in the first period. Each time, I haul myself up again. I keep smiling and cheering on all my teammates—including Hunter—even when I totally want to give up.

As the game goes on, I realize I have a much better feel for the ice than I did last year. All that time in net has improved my skills—and helped me see things differently.

The score stays knotted at zero until the end of the third period. There can't be a tie in the semifinals, so the game goes into overtime. "Five minutes stop time," the ref explains, "and then the shoot-out."

Everyone looks at Hunter, who smiles. "I got this. You think I haven't learned a thing or two from watching Jelly play net?"

I smile back, glad my jealousy didn't totally ruin things between Hunter and me. Maybe he just needed a win of his own. Or a lucky bobblehead to give him the confidence he needs.

I lean against the boards so I can feel the piece of bobblehead in my side pocket. For a second I wish I still had the whole thing, just in case I have to be in the shoot-out. Like Grandpa said, there's nothing wrong with asking for help. At this point, though, I really believe I can do it on my own.

I'm tired but determined. When I get out for my first over-time shift, I skate as if it's game seven of the Olympics. The play switches direction at least four times, but no one on either team gets the puck near the net.

"CHANGE," Coach Lisa calls. Madder skates for the bench, but Charlie and I are caught on the far side as the opposing team gobbles up the puck and storms into our zone. I chase the play, hoping to break up the three-on-two.

The player with the puck goes in deep, with too much speed, and can't get a shot away. I skate behind the net to challenge him but fall trying to stop. He digs the puck out from under me and passes it to the front of the net. His teammate takes a shot. Hunter kicks the puck away. It skitters toward the red face-off spot.

Scrambling, I get to the puck first.

"Outlet pass to Charlie!" Duncan screams.

I swat the puck in Charlie's direction. He picks it up and stickhandles down the middle. Mouse is on the ice in place of Madder. Our lines are completely messed up, and I'm not sure where to go. Waiting till Charlie crosses the blue line, I charge for the net, even though I'm sucking enough wind to create a vacuum.

Just as he's about to lose control of the puck, Charlie takes a shot. The puck bounces off the goalie. Mouse pokes at the rebound, sending it across the crease to the open side of the net.

I watch it hit the post in slow motion. It bounces off and comes straight at me.

As I reach for it, I get shoved from behind. I'm off-balance, but I don't lose sight of the puck. Before their defense can get a stick on it, I bury it with a backhand—something I've done a million times in mini sticks, but not once on the ice.

It's my first minor-hockey goal.

CHAPTER 40

There are no Player of the Game awards in this tournament. But after the overtime victory, my teammates wrap me in toilet paper, chanting "MVP" as the last notes of our win song fill the dressing room.

I don't feel like the most valuable player, but I do feel like the most versatile—Mom might say *resilient* as well. Being accepted by my teammates for who I am is worth a million times more than the award I got at the last tournament.

ELLIOT FELDNER-MARTEL

Jelly GOALIE

TRAIL BLAZERS

The win gets us into the finals, setting up a championship rematch between the Blazers and the Coyotes. With less than an hour between games, Dad buys me a burger at the concession stand. He doesn't even hint that I should try the chicken pita wrap or anything else "healthy."

"Is it your turn in net, E?" Dad asks when I've polished off the iced tea he bought me to go with it.

"Yes. But no," I say. "Hunter's starting."

Dad raises his eyebrows. "And you're okay with that?'

To be honest, I wasn't happy when Coach Tibor pulled Hunter and me aside after the last game to tell us. I'm nervous about facing number 16—the Coyote who called me a bender and a sieve. What if I lose my temper again?

But with a full stomach and Dad's support, I'm feeling okay about Coach Tibor's decision now. "Hunter's a better goalie," I say to Dad. "And besides, I can play out. He can't. His dad won't let him."

Dad rubs his chin. "So you think you'll have a better chance at winning with Hunter in net?"

"I guess. But winning isn't everything," I say. And I mean it.

It's not just because of what Dad said after Aislyn got third place in the contest. Or because of what Mom said after losing the election. I'm actually starting to believe I don't have to win to fit in—not just on my team, but as part of my family as well. Being the best isn't nearly as important as being myself.

"I just want to contribute to my team in any way I can. And have fun."

Dad smiles. "I'm proud of you, E."

With Hunter dressed in his goalie gear and me in the player equipment I've scraped together, we gather around Jerry-Horn so he can lead the team cheer. "Let's win this for Elliot," he says. "Let's be there for him the way he's been there for us. In and out of net."

I look around the circle at my friends. Duncan, Jerry-Horn, Fartsby, Madder, Kali, Gray, Charlie, Mouse, Hunter—they all contribute to the team in their own ways.

"Let's do this for all of us." I put my hand in the middle to join the others. "For the Blazers!"

"One, two, three—"

"BLAZERS!" We raise our hands in unison.

"Time to grill some cheese," Jerry-Horn yells.

We lose 4–3.

Coach Matt calls it a heartbreaker. Coach Tibor calls it the best game we've ever played. Coach Lisa calls for a rematch. "One tournament for us and one for them. The next one is OURS!"

The Blazers don't face the Coyotes again, though. We split our last six games of the season (three wins, three losses) to finish third in our division, ahead of the other Trail teams. In the playoffs we battle hard—Hunter and I taking turns in net—but go down with an overtime loss in the semis.

"You gonna play next year, Jelly?" Hunter asks as he digs the ball out from behind the shooter tutor attached to the front of the net in Duncan's garage. The street's too full of gravel from the spring runoff and the basement is too small for four of us to play.

"Of course," I say. "I've been raking lawns to earn money for registration fees."

"In net or out?" asks Gray, my partner in our two-on-two matchup.

"I haven't decided yet." A lot of decisions have been made in the last couple of months. Mom's running in a municipal by-election for city councillor, Aislyn's already picked a project for next year's contest, and Dad's decided to teach a woods class at the college this summer. But I'm keeping my options open. I've already earned money to pay for a figure-skating clinic. Plus I'm signed up for a goalie camp that offers discounted rates for new goaltenders.

"What about you?" Duncan asks Hunter as he takes a pass from him.

"Dad still wants to kill me for not playing spring league," he says. "But I'm not trying out for rep. I like playing house league. And I don't need the extra competition—it turns me into someone I don't want to be."

No one's sure how to respond, so we concentrate on the play. Duncan fakes a shot and passes back to Hunter. Gray thrusts his stick forward to intercept the pass but just misses. Hunter shoots. The ball brushes one of the small openings in the tarp and bounces off.

I collect the ball and stickhandle to the other side of the garage. "I know what you mean, Hunter. Sometimes I think the best part of hockey is this part."

"What part?" asks Duncan.

"Just playing. With friends."

ACKNOWLEDGMENTS

Heaps of gratitude to my son, Spencer. Without the hours I spent watching you on the ice, I never would have dreamed up Elliot's story. (And I still wouldn't have any idea what really goes on in the dressing room!) To both Oliver and Spencer, thank you so much for your feedback and support during every stage of writing this book. I couldn't—and wouldn't—have done it without you.

I'm very lucky to have amazing critique partners, including David Wright and Miriam Spitzer Franklin. Thank you both for your feedback on early drafts of this story, and thank you, Miriam, for helping with the pitch. I also have the *best* writing support group *ever*. My eternal gratitude to Samika Swift, Christine Thomas Alderman and Jerry Mikorenka—you are all gifted writers and great friends.

Big thanks to Tanya Trafford, who acquired this story just before Carey Price led the Montreal Canadiens to the Stanley Cup Finals in 2021. Together we cheered him on and made Elliot's story stronger. I learned so much from you, Tanya, and I can't tell you how much I appreciate your editorial eye and encouragement to trust my instincts. And to the rest of the team at Orca Book Publishers—thank you for the opportunity to work with you again.

Even though we've never met, a big shout-out to Carey Price himself. Thank you for being such an excellent role model for young people like Elliot. Organized sport needs more heroes like you.

Writing is hard, and I couldn't do it without my circle of support. Thank you to all my friends who picked me up when I was feeling down. Thank you to my mom and sister for cheering me on over our weekly, virtual tea breaks. And thank you to my stepdad, who will never get used to how long it takes a book to become a book (because he's always so anxious to read them!).

Last but never least, I would not be a writer if it wasn't for my husband, Tim. Thank you for everything.

Read on for
an excerpt from

MY
BEST FRIEND
IS EXTINCT

by Rebecca Wood Barrett

Henry loves the snow. When his town receives a record-breaking snowfall, he's absolutely thrilled. Then one day, while exploring one of the many tunnels running through the town's snowbanks, Henry discovers a strange, prehistoric-like creature. His classmates don't believe him but Henry knows something is out there.

I wasn't supposed to play outside yet, but searching for the Thing was more important than following the rules. Besides, my head felt fine.

I grabbed a flashlight, duct tape, a shovel, two granola bars, cheese strings, a mini Kit Kat left over from Halloween, a thermos of soup, my water bottle and a rope my mom used to tie stuff to the roof rack of the car. Then I quickly made a peanut-butter-and-jam sandwich and crammed everything into my backpack. I pulled out my snow gear, including a pair of tinted ski goggles to cut down the brightness of the snow. Mom would be proud that I was being so responsible. I also wrote her a note so she wouldn't worry.

Dear Mom,

I am on an expedishun to explore the local snowbanks. Dont worry I have packed supplies and my head is ok. If I am not home in time for desert send help.

Love, Henry

I was pretty sure the creature wouldn't eat me, but you never know.

Whenever possible, I take the shortcut. They often turn out to be longcuts, but they're usually more exciting. So instead of taking the boring route around our lane, I headed directly for the pyramid of packed ice dumped between houses. Beyond that were a few fir trees, the snowbank and the main road.

I climbed three steps only to slide back down again. I needed an ice ax. A stick would have worked, but the whole world was buried under snow, so finding one would be a challenge. I looked around and spotted one of the bright orange snow markers that showed where the boulders and fire hydrants

and electrical boxes were so the snowplow didn't hit them. I grabbed a marker and yanked it out.

It worked like a charm. I plunged my new fluorescent ice ax into the ice wall and climbed upward. When I got to the top, I threw it down the other side like a spear so I could use it for my return climb.

As I started to slide down the back side of the pyramid, I realized I should have hung on to the ax for a bit longer. I dug in my heels, but that didn't slow me down. I was headed straight for a tree! I braced for impact, but my boots slipped to either side, and I sacked myself on the tree trunk.

To make things worse, the impact caused a slab of snow to fall from the branches above and bomb me with powder. When I could move again, I stood up and shook myself like a dog. Despite the pain, I was grateful I'd hit this tree instead of flying off the cliff.

Fortunately the snow around the tree well had mostly been packed down by the heavy stuff that had been pushed in by the snowplow, so the tree well wasn't too deep. Mom has always warned me about tree wells. If you fall into a big one, it's almost impossible to climb out without help. I pushed off the hard-packed snow at the bottom and rolled out on my side through the fluffier new snow.

I took a few steps around the tree and stood at the edge of the cliff. There was a massive, powdery snowbank at the bottom that ran alongside the street. Now I was sorry I had hit the tree. Not that I'd had a choice. But I should have slid past, flown into the air and landed on that beautiful, thick mattress of snow.

I was about to leap off when I remembered I had a rope in my backpack. A jump would be quicker but climbing down the cliff face—now that would be an adventure! I tied the rope around the now familiar tree trunk and leaned away from it, feeding the rope through my mitts. At the edge of the cliff, I leaned way back and hopped off.

I pushed off the wall of the cliff with my boots three times before I lost my grip on the rope. I plummeted to the bottom and smacked into the snowbank. I lay there for a brief second, and then *whoof*, I somehow fell into it.

I landed on a hard surface. Chunks of hard snow rained down on me, and a fine mist of ice crystals floated in the air. I looked around and realized I was in a carved-out space of some kind. My heart sped up, and my chest tightened with fear. Would it collapse and crush me? I took a deep breath the way Mom told me to when I get nervous. *Breathe in. Breathe out. Breathe in. Breathe out.* My heart slowed down.

The ceiling hadn't collapsed.

I was fine.

The hole above me let in a little light. I made a snowball and tossed it to get a sense of how big this space was. It disappeared in the darkness. I wriggled my backpack off and pulled out my flashlight. When I turned it on, I was amazed to discover I was in a tunnel. This one was much bigger than the tunnel we'd made at school. I could stand up without hitting my head. Stretching out my arms, my fingers just touched the sides. The walls of snow had a blue tinge like the inside of a glacier.

I held out the flashlight and strained to see. My light only shone on the area about twenty steps ahead of me, and beyond that it was dark. Who or what had made this tunnel? There was no way it could have formed naturally. And there was no way I was not going to explore it.

Suddenly I heard a *whoosh*ing noise. And it was getting louder. What if it was the creature swishing along the tunnel, coming to get me? I prepared myself for attack as the sound got closer and closer. And then it was right on top of me! The tunnel shook, and I cowered on the floor. My heart pounded. But the noise passed. It must have been a car. Out on the road. There was no sign of the creature.

That didn't mean it wasn't waiting out there in the dark. But I had to find out. As I inched up the tunnel, I heard nothing but the sound of my breathing and the rustle of my jacket and snow pants. I felt the hair stand up on the back of my neck. Mom always said to pay attention if your spidey senses started tingling. Even though I couldn't see or hear anything, I just knew something was there.

I kept going. Faster. I saw a sudden flash of white fur up ahead. The Thing! I knew it. And it was running away from me! I forgot how terrified I'd felt only minutes before. I started to chase after it.

I followed at full tilt. My breath punched in and out until my lungs felt like they would pop. I was just about to give up when the creature stopped and flopped over. *What?*

Something was clearly wrong with it.

Maybe it was sick or injured. I had to help. Carefully I inched toward it. I could see its belly heaving up and down.

The animal lifted its head and blinked at me. I froze. I had never seen anything like it. Pale blue eyes, the same color as the walls of snow, shone in the light. Covered in thick white fur, the creature had faint gray stripes above its eyes and two triangular ears poking out from the top of its head. It reminded me of a mash-up of a polar bear and something out of Dr. Seuss with its huge oversized paws, long skinny legs and a short snout like a lion's.

Something about those eyes made me unfreeze. I was still a little scared, but I had this urge to stick my hands in the creature's fur and give it a pat. When I got close enough to touch it, I took off my gloves. I reached out to stroke it. Underneath

its fur I could feel a bone poking out. A low growl rumbled in its throat.

"I won't hurt you," I said.

Suddenly it snapped at me, its teeth scraping over the back of my hand. I yelped and flew backward, landing on my backpack. I rolled over and sat up. The creature lowered its head and shut its eyes. Was it dying? Or maybe it was starving.

"Poor guy," I said in a soft voice. "Are you hungry?"

A threatening growl was the answer. The back of my hand throbbed. Under the glare of the flashlight, I could see two long red scrapes.

But I still felt like I needed to help. I opened my backpack and took out my thermos. I unscrewed the lid and filled it to the brim with water. Then I pushed the lid toward the mouth of the creature, until my arm was within snapping distance. Would it chomp my hand again?

I nudged the lid closer. The white head didn't move. I poked the lid again and again, until it was inches from the tip of the animal's black nose. I waited. Nothing happened.

"Here's a little bit of water for you."

A weak growl.

A sniff. White whiskers quivered. A pink tongue slipped out sideways and dipped into the lid, scooping in the water and then sliding back into the creature's mouth. The tongue moved like it had a mind of its own, separate from the animal, which didn't budge or open its eyes. After a minute the tongue had slurped up all the liquid it could reach, and it disappeared back into the mouth.

"More water?" I asked.

The creature gave a huge yawn and said, "Yarp."

I was stunned. *Yarp?* Was that a yawn, or the word *yes*? I reached out hesitantly for the lid and stopped midway. Was this a trick? Would the creature snatch my hand and try to eat me? I could tell it was definitely thirsty. Hungry too, by the looks of it. I leaned in closer. That was when I noticed the bloody, matted wound on its front leg, between its big paw and knee.

I grabbed the lid, filled it and thrust it near the animal's snout. The nose twitched.

"Here you go. More water."

The animal lapped it up, this time with more enthusiasm. Maybe the first drink had brought it back to life. When the water was all gone, I asked, "More water?"

"Yarp."

"Yarp," I said filling the lid again. This time I didn't bother to pull my hand away.

This went on for a while, me filling the lid, the white creature lapping up the water, me offering more and him saying *yarp*. As it lay on its side, I took a closer look and decided it was definitely a male. By the time I ran out of water, he was holding his head up. When he was finished he tilted his head at me.

"It's gone. You drank it all."

He put his head down between his paws and gave his wound a weak lick, then lay still and closed his eyes.

I had no idea what kind of food this guy ate, but luckily I'd come prepared for a major expedition. I hauled out a couple of sticks of string cheese and peeled off the plastic, then ripped the cheese into small hunks. I took one for myself. The rest I plopped in front of his nose.

A whisker twitch. A sniff. His tongue tapped the cheese and then scooped it up into his mouth. He didn't chew much, just snarfed up the chunks in seconds. When he was done he gave a little whine. I poured some soup into the thermos lid, and he slurped that up too. Before long he'd eaten everything I'd brought in my pack. While he was munching, I took a closer look at his wound. There was a dried crust around the edge, a flap of skin missing and some dark holes. They looked like tooth marks.

"This is not good." I pointed at the wound. "We need to clean that and get a bandage on it, or it won't heal. We should go back to my house, and I can wrap it up."

He licked the wound again, then sniffed the air.

"You ate all the food. I'll have to go home to get more."

He looked down the tunnel, his blue eyes opening wide. A whine escaped his lips. He lurched, trying to get to his feet, but his long legs wobbled weakly, and he slumped down again.

I heard a scraping noise like an earthquake rolling toward us. In one last fearful effort, the creature managed to stand and take a step, then fell into my lap.

Yolanda Ridge is the author of the middle-grade novel *Inside Hudson Pickle* and the juvenile nonfiction title *CRISPR: A Powerful Way to Change DNA*, both of which were Junior Library Guild Gold Standard Selections. She has also written two environment-themed novels for the Orca Young Readers line, *Trouble in the Trees* and *Road Block*. She has a master of science degree and is adept at making complex concepts understandable—a skill she uses in her writing, teaching and author visits. She lives in Rossland, British Columbia.

Sydney Barnes is an illustrator and book designer with a lifelong passion for books. She illustrated the children's book *Painted Fences*. She holds a master of publishing degree from Simon Fraser University and runs a design business called SJBarnes Design. She lives in Victoria, British Columbia.